Sink or Swim

A collection of short stories

KEPRESSNG

NIGERIA | UK

First Published in Nigeria in 2024 by Kemka Ezinwo Press Ltd.
First Published in the United Kingdom in 2024 by Kepressng Ltd.

The moral rights of the authors has been asserted.
Individual contributions ©2024

This book is sold subject to the condition that it shall not, by way of trade or otherwise, be lent, re-sold, hired out or otherwise circulated without the publisher's prior written consent in any form of binding or cover other than that it is published and without a similar condition including this condition being imposed on the subsequent purchaser.

Kemka Ezinwo Press Ltd (KEP) has no control over or responsibility for any author or third-party websites or articles that may be referred to in or on this book.

A CIP catalogue record for this book is available from the Nigerian National Library & the British Library.

ISBN: 978-978-60784 -0-3 (Paperback)
ISBN: 978-978-60784 -1-0 (E-Book)

This novel is entirely a work of fiction. The names, characters, and incidents portrayed in it are the work of the author's imagination. Any resemblance to actual persons, living or dead, events or localities is entirely coincidental.

Typeset by Kepressng Ltd
Cover design by Agnes Kay-E.

To
GOD
All the writers who made this book possible.

CONTENTS

SINK OR SWIM 7
AJEJI 49
HOW KINGS ARE MADE 67
UNHOLY MATRIMONY 83
A BUNCH OF JARGONS 98
TO KILL A SINGLE YORUBA WOMAN 113
SOLVED 135
THE FIRST DAY TICKET 157
THE VISIT 179
MALI 192
TUG OF DEFIANCE 206
DUMB LUCK 224
CONTACTS 257
OTHER TITLES 258
ABOUT US 259
2026 COMPETITION 260

SINK OR SWIM

- Agnes Kay-E

Adonye-Ake, a fishing village of eighteen families built on stilts over water, is the smallest and most congenial of the eight hamlets of Korokorosei. The house closest to the sea's awning had long taken a dive, and the house was leaning precariously close to the water. It belonged to Peresuotei's late wife, Ine, and had been passed down to her by her great-grandfather, Suo.

Suo, a well-known rifle maker in his time, married eleven wives, but only his first wife bore him a daughter, who in turn bore his only granddaughter. He had seen his great-granddaughter before he passed, and he outlived the generations after him, except his great-granddaughter.

Peresuotei smacked his lips as he yearned for *kaikai*. He'd drank the last dregs a few hours ago. He glanced at his daughter, who was huddled up in one corner of the room, asleep. Craving the familiar burn of *kaikai*, he stepped out of his house, stumbling and made his way down his window onto Seigha's awning, down the ladder, waiting for a canoe.

Peresuotei raised a dispassionate brow when Seigha bent over one of the stilts, tapping it and shaking his head. Seigha was Peresuotei's neighbour and best friend since childhood.

"I'll fix it," Peresuotei mumbled disdainfully.

"I've been hearing that," Seigha countered, unimpressed and concerned. "Your procrastination is sea wide."

"I'll fix it," Peresuotei insisted, irritated. Seigha was always intrusive, objecting to his selling his canoes and indulging in *kaikai,* but he'd not listened and could barely hold onto a canoe for more than once a week. He was afraid to admit to his best friend that he'd sold the remaining one last night to the portly owner of the *kaikai* spot he frequented.

"You're blest with only one child. You should be able to keep her safe."

"I know," Peresuotei replied dismissively, then added, "Are you coming with me?"

Seigha slanted his head to glance at the burnt orange sun that had cast its soft glow over the calm surface of the endless expanse of water as it descended and wrinkled his nose.

"Do you have to go?" Seigha asked.

Peresuotei shrugged, jumping onto a canoe heading towards the Swali hamlet, the only hamlet that freely sold *kaikai*.

"*Kurotimibai*," Seigha sighed, but the canoe had gone a distance. He stared at the canoe until it was a speck.

Ebiye, Peresuotei's daughter, stared out of the window of her weather-beaten house; the floor was damp and cold under her feet. She had stopped complaining about the dilapidation of their abode, making the best of what she had - her mother's old clothes, her father's unusable fishnets and the two broad, sturdy sticks she'd salvaged during a flood from a couple of years ago.

Ebiye had over time combated her hunger by singing and dreaming of food and a good place to sleep. Sometimes, she'd have a conversation with the sticks. She'd even grown accustomed to her father's absence since her mother passed six years ago; her father only stumbled into the house when the moon shifted to give way to the sun.

"*Serido*," she'd greet him whenever she found him in the morning. Or "Nua'o" whenever he returned during the day, with some food for her, which had gotten rarer. Seigha tossed food through the window once a week. She'd learnt to stand by the window to catch it before it ended up on the floor with a splat.

The women in Adonye-Ake weren't seen outside the houses except on market days and nuptials. On such occasions, there would be music, copious laughter and loads of chatter spewing out of every awning as mothers and daughters emerged from their dwellings in throngs to find out what they'd missed and then get on their canoes where they'd dance and sing until they got to the market town.

The market days were the ultimate social gathering outside weddings. The women dressed up to show off their husbands' wealth by accentuating the curves of their bodies, the weight of their strides, the sheen of their skin, and even their hairstyles. Their popularity, however, was based on the girth of their waist, the size of their breasts once they became mothers, the number of children they had, the girth of their daughter's bottom and the smooth curve of their daughter's legs.

The women who came to buy their fish, crayfish, or any other from-the-sea wares came early before the men converged as they'll generally not haggle because their real intention was to appraise a suitable bride based on status and appeal in the guise of buying.

Ebiye was always absent from these events. She longed to be part of it. She had no one to teach her how to skillet a fish, string them into a loop or stack them in a stick. She longed to be seen, to be chosen as a bride, to be paraded as a new bride to the fattening room at the other end of their hamlet but she had no chaperone. Her mother, when alive, was sickly and the folks believed it was because of her great-grandfather's enterprise.

The hunger began to spread as the catches dwindled. Disillusioned and idle, the men found solace in *kaikai,* and the maidens grew older with no suitor to stake a claim. There was unease as the mouths to feed multiplied.

As the maidens were determined to marry men who would cater for their would-be children, they refused to marry within their hamlet because the men lacked ambition; most of them had begun to follow their father's footsteps, indulging in drinking and doing nothing else – The women yearned for an outlet, for with no seafood to sell they couldn't leave their houses. More so, the industrious maidens felt trapped.

There was a rumour about the Suotei, a land beyond Zuo, the central market of hamlets. It was uninhabited.

It was also believed that it was endowed with lush, fertile grounds, towering trees and fragrant plants that made perfect shade for sweltering heat, and several streams of fresh water. The only way across was by canoe but the water was made treacherous by sea monsters.

Amidst the apprehension and fears, Ebikeme, twice a widow, was determined to find industrious men for her daughters or make Suotei a home for them; though faced with scepticism and scorn she was undeterred.

"Nengi," she started conspiratorially when her sister came to take more food from her. "I will go to Suotei."

Alarmed, Nengi cried, "Ata! Don't say that!"

"Look at our children." Ebikeme gestured. "You had to sneak in here to get food for them. How long do you think this will last?"

Nengi shook her head vehemently.

"These young men are becoming more forceful, towing the path of their fathers..." she sighed dramatically. "Doing nothing better than drowning themselves in *kaikai.*"

"Stop saying things like that," Nengi admonished and waved her hand over her head to ward off the evil in her sister's words. "Besides, what will your in-laws say?"

"What do you think? They said no but they are men."

"Please stop this," Nengi pleaded.

"You would understand if you had daughters," Ebikeme sighed heavily as she handed Nengi a basket full of yam, fish, crayfish and salt.

"Thank you," Nengi sighed, her gratitude palpable. "Please, stop saying these things."

"I have to," Ebikeme said, more determined. "They call me names during the day and seek my bed at night. But you won't understand, Nengi, your husband is beside you."

Nengi smiled ruefully. "You mean with a myriad of wives alongside."

She will never understand, Ebikeme thought, shaking her head.

That night, while her daughters were asleep, she packed her bags. The following morning, she told her daughters her plan and what their uncles had said. On the other hand, she was worried about her best friend's daughter, Ebiye.

Her daughters assured her that they'd follow the tradition until she returned for them.

Soon after, she stepped out to the awning and waited for canoes – she was allowed that leeway because she ran her own business and a lot of people relied on her canoes, including her in-laws.

"*Serido,*" Ebikeme greeted one of her employees who was busy mooring her canoe while struggling to steady his drunk passenger – Peresuotei.

"Peresuotei, I need to talk to you.

Peresuotei, staggered, chuckling.

"I'm going to Suotei," Ebikeme said, her voice tinged with desperation and urgency.

Peresuotei's eyes bulged in surprise, followed by a hearty laugh.

"I want your daughter to come with me."

Peresuotei laughed even harder.

"You know she is better off with me."

Peresuotei staggered and waved his hand at an approaching canoe, burped and asked, "What about your daughters?"

Ebikeme's shoulders slumped. "My in-laws won't let me."

"Why would you think I'll want her to go?"

"She'll have no one to help her. She needs an industrious husband," Ebikeme pressed. "How many times have you fed her without my help?"

"We'll manage," Peresuotei said with a wave of his hand.

"You know she'll be better off with me," she pleaded.

"No. No, Ebikeme," Peresuotei slurred. "I cannot allow my daughter to go with you. She deserves a clean name."

Ebikeme's heart sank but determined she asked, "How will she be fed? Who will feed her?"

"We'll manage," he repeated and climbed into Seigha's boat.

"*Serido*," Seigha murmured cheerfully as his canoe approached.

"*Serido*," Ebikeme said while Peresuotei burped.

"Ebikeme, are you still going to Suotei?"

"Yes. Our daughters need good men. Besides, there are no fishes in our river."

Seigha nodded. "Go well."

"*Nua'o*," Ebikeme greeted the occupants of an approaching canoe, but they averted their gazes.

The next day before the tide shifted, she left with two out of her three canoes.

Ebikeme lost her canoes to two groups of hooligans barely an hour after arriving at the shores of the other end of the bustling market clan of Zuo. It had taken her four days to get there by the in-rivers. Fortunately, they had tossed her bags of wares, containing her fishing and farming tools and food; they'd fumbled with the covering that Timadi and Timieri had made from old fishing nets and bamboo and discarded them in frustration.

Every canoe that was towed by human hands had enough people for it, and they were reluctant to take women. One man remained on shore because he needed a passenger. He was old, half-blind and half deaf. There were no other canoes except his battered one.

"*Nua'o*! Are you going to Suotei?"

"You're a woman," he sighed.

"Yes."

"That's unfortunate. I'm going to Suotei, but I'm not carrying a woman."

She frowned; her hope deflating and then annoyed, she retorted, "Do you need someone to swing your oars or not?"

"You're not a man," he insisted after she pleaded. "I don't want you to nag me when you get tired. I've had enough of that in my house."

She raised a brow, suspecting the man was running away from his family and responsibilities:

"You'll need someone to cook, clean –"

"No, I don't," he said and turned his back to her.

She sat on the sand, staring at the endless sea. She heard the old man's stomach rumble and smiled. She'd taken a look at his canoe earlier and knew he had nothing in it. She slanted her head to her bag but didn't know if he was a greedy person - she didn't want anyone to know she had food in the bags.

Wanting to prove her usefulness if only to get her to Suotei, she decided to make something for them to eat without going through her bags. She walked along the plain beach until she found two long twigs, bound them together with a knotted string from an old fishing net and added one of the hooks she used to repair her late husband's fishing nets to it. And then she trudged to a raised ground with less sand and swung the improvised fishing line.

She guffawed at the instant catch and struggled to hold it steady, but as she began to pull, it got loose. She picked up her hook and gasped. She gawked at the hook; it had a bite mark, and half of it was gone.

While contemplating what could have caused it, sharp sounds pierced the air. It only lasted a few seconds, but a sense of foreboding washed over her, and she knew that if she hung around a little longer, she wouldn't have the courage to continue on the journey. She was already seen as a hag because she didn't value the traditions of her clan, so if she returned empty-handed, her daughters wouldn't stand a chance when the mockery began.

"Well," the man mumbled. "Let's go."

She raised a brow at him.

"If you're joining me, you'll not nag or say anything throughout the journey."

A little confused, she pointed to herself with raised brows.

"Give me your word," the man demanded impatiently.

"I will not say anything throughout the journey," she replied with a smile. It was easy enough; she'd had years of practice.

Ebikeme hurled her bags onto his canoe but became

somewhat concerned; the water reached the ream when they boarded. The old man feigned tiredness when it was time to row, but she took the oars off him without complaining. The water was calm, and she hoped it would remain so until she got to Suotei.

The old man murmured his plans for what he'd do when he arrived there, but she refused to dream of the beauty of the place.

They'd been in the water for some time before she began to hear gurgling. The water was still, where there were supposed to be waves of ripples from her rowing. The gurgling got louder and stronger the closer she got to the other canoes. The old man began to hum the sound, too. The canoes were empty and moored by each other, making it hard for them to pass through. She heard a few more voices humming the sound but couldn't tell where they were coming from due to the number of canoes.

Ebikeme's arms ached. She wanted to rest, but when she saw one of the first canoes she'd seen when she arrived at Zuo, she nudged their canoe a little closer. She had liked the canoe because of its size, though thought the reflective shards of crystal coating its outer body obnoxious, the owner had explained that he'd woken up to find that his daughter had spent all night doing it.

She was about to rest her hands when she caught a movement in the water. It struck her as odd because their canoe didn't move, nor were there any extraordinary ripples around them, which would be normal if there'd been a big fish close by. Assuming it was an illusion caused by pangs of hunger, she shook her head and continued rowing until they were stuck between others.

Marooned, Ebikeme decided to wait for strength to return to her arms. While waiting, she got up to stretch her legs, and as she did, she realised that the canoes were tightly packed, so much so that she could climb onto one, and it wouldn't wobble. Curious, she leapt onto other canoes, seeking survivors to find out about the creature and possibly how to defeat it.

To her surprise, there was no sound coming out of the big canoe; it had dozens of people on it when they left the shore. It also stood apart from the others.

The screeching sounds, though beneath her, were now much louder and had begun to hurt her ears. The old man was now standing when she got to the area of the sea that had the most canoes. She heard a different humming from behind her. A few minutes later, she heard more, way up ahead, as if it was forming a circle around her.

Suspecting it could be a trap, she hurried back to the old man's canoe and instinctively rowed towards the big one if only to keep her ahead of all the moored canoes, but as she did, she felt several nudges underneath them. She rowed faster. The old man staggered and fell on his buttocks and began to rock the canoe in tandem with the creature beneath them as he sang louder.

It is only attacking canoes that's moving, she thought but saw a woman struggling to untangle her canoe steadily move forward and suspected it was picking the ones that people were singing. She smiled, relieved that Ebiye had not followed her. Perhaps if Ebiye had, she would have tied her mouth.

"Whatever is calling you, it's not taking me," she muttered under her breath as she got up, raised an oar to pull the big canoe closer and hooked the oar to a large rope on its side. She stretched her free hand to nudge her bags to her and piled them on the ends of the oar. With her bags now secure on both ends of the oar, she pushed it high above her but struggled to make it slip into the mirrored canoe.

She called the old man to help, but her voice seemed to irritate him because he rocked their canoe harder, weakening her grip. A few seconds later, something struck her canoe, causing it to careen away from the big one, and in trying to keep her balance, she staggered forward into the old man who was propelled in her direction by what had knocked their canoe. Massaging her head, she held onto the seat in the canoe.

The canoe was rocked harder from beneath again, sending shivers down her spine. The big canoe was now a good distance away, and her canoe was getting away from the others. Struck by a feeling that the creature was shielding the big canoe from the others as no other canoe was close to it, she stood up. Without thinking, she took big leaps onto other canoes, falling into some but continued hopping until she got close to the big one.

She looked at the distance between her and the big canoe in despair. It wasn't safe enough to swim towards it. She couldn't leave her food and tools, which had been knocked into it, behind because there was no land on the horizon. Worse still, most of the canoes around her had lost their oars, and it was getting dark. If she lost track of her path on the moonless night, it would be hard to know where she was heading.

She glanced back at the old man who was still swaying to the song only he could hear. She discovered two more canoes with people; one had a man who'd tied himself to his canoe, and another had a plump woman perched on a man struggling to get into the water. It was then that it dawned on her. The unheard song was affecting only the men.

She asked the woman if she could help as they were closer to her, but the woman glared at her, so she turned her attention back to the big canoe. She picked a discarded oar and used it to nudge a canoe towards the big one as she figured, if she could make a beeline with them then she could run towards it.

The canoe was nudged back, but she tried again, and this time, nudging more than one so that one went through, and she did it again until it was almost a complete path, then one got nudged out of the way from beneath the water. Determined, she continued as she figured if the monster couldn't stop her from beneath the water, now it was a matter of time before it would get angry enough to skid to the surface.

That big canoe held something the monster didn't like or couldn't handle, and it would be her ticket to the other side. She had gone past exhaustion and wanted to continue her journey while she was still awake as the canoe could be turned off course and she'd get lost while she slept.

While she tried to line up other canoes, a sharp cry jolted her out of exhaustion. She turned to find the woman and the man she'd tried to help plunge into the swirling whirlpool beside them. The water became calm at that end, but a new whirlpool was formed beside the old man's canoe.

"Watch out!" she cried, but the old man didn't seem to hear her.

A few more whirlpools were forming around the edges of the huddled canoes. She felt the water move beneath her.

"Something is following me," she whispered and began to run, not caring that one of the canoes had been knocked off. Her heart pounded so much that she shook her head a couple of times to stay focused.

Just as she began to climb into the big one, the one she stood on was pulled down, causing her to fall forward against the big canoe. She quickly gripped the oar she had used earlier and lifted herself until she was high enough to hook a leg on the twine.

She began to sigh with relief when the water beside her began to whirl into a descending pool.

"Iye," she cried and scrambled into the canoe just as a grey creature twice her height and size leapt out of the water. On its back was a map of wavy lines reminding her of mackerels, its mouth widening, revealing rows of jagged teeth. It was a grotesque fusion of woman and fish.

Shaking, she closed her eyes and felt her body to find out if the creature had made off with any part. She'd sustained several cuts from the reflective flat stones outside it but was relieved. She heard more cries and sheltered her ears.

There was nothing in the canoe except herself and her bags. Luckily, their oars were bigger at the ends, each attached through a hole, which made it impossible to get loose unless broken. She contemplated how she would row an eight-oared canoe as they were far apart.

She had to come up with a way to guide the canoe to the other side, she thought as she glanced at the setting sun. She missed her children. Wondered if they were still resisting the boys of the community and leering men who remained unfaithful to their numerous wives.

It had been a month since Ebikeme left Adonye-Ake for Suotei. The waters underneath the houses had risen due to days of heavy downpours. In the house closest to the sea, Peresuotei's daughter, Ebiye, tried to sleep through the unsettling creaks of her tilted abode.

Ebiye so sighed with relief when the rain finally stopped to reveal the sun that she sang an ode:

> Cast your warmth to dry this floor.
> Cast your warmth to thaw these walls.
> Hide no more behind dark clouds.
> Smile to me,
> And I'll sing to you.

> When you left, the rain came down.
> So much so my house now creaks.
> The stilts are weak and giving in.
> Warm this house,
> And I'll sing to you.

> My tremors, gifts of cold and fear.
> The rising sea warns my home.
> I know this house on stilts won't stand.
> Shine brightly,
> And I'll sing to you.

> Fishing nets strung to the windows,
> All my singing, none had come.
> Sole and lonely, I know no one.
> I'm sinking fast,
> Will you still hear me?

No fattening rooms or market days.
I'll never be called 'Iye'.
I am all pipe dreams and failed hopes.
If I could swim,
Will you make me glow?

Great, hot and yellow crystal stay,
Keep me warm,
And I'll sing to you.

It was almost evening before Ebiye was lulled to sleep by another hunger pang, but it didn't last. Her father had not yet returned, so she leaned against the window, singing as she waited hopefully for Seigha's offering and trying not to stare at the other half of the house now submerged in water.

When she could no longer bear the water lapping against the wall of the house, she tied the ends of her father's discarded fishing net to the windows and sat on them, clutching tightly to her sticks. Her father had not returned in days, and she anxiously hoped he hadn't fallen into the sea in a drunken stupor.

She watched helplessly as the food Seigha had thrown through her window fell into the submerged section of the house. Bubbles emerged with a sudden gust of air, and Ebiye felt herself sinking.

In a frantic bid for survival, she twirled the sticks that had become her companion around her father's discarded fishing nets and hung onto them. The remnants of Seigha's kindness scattered as fishes tugged at it.

In the house next door, Seigha sat on the floor, bent over two large bowls, his fingers curled around a large morsel of *garri* when he felt a tremor - it had been happening for days. This quake was different; it rocked his house, and it was quickly followed by the sound that occurred when a canoe capsized.

"What was that?" he asked curiously, his hand hovering in mid-air. He listened for the warning bell, but hearing nothing, he lowered his head and began to eat.

"The singing has stopped," his wife mumbled distractedly and dipped her hand in the soup to take a piece of fish.

He swatted her hand away as he said, "Not that!"

Shrugging, his wife padded to the window to shut it as a big gust of wind pushed it open.

"Seigha," she gasped. "Seigha," she repeated loudly. "Your friend's house – it's gone into the sea."

Seigha laughed dismissively, shaking his head and digging up more fish with his morsel of *garri*.

"Seigha!" she called again, sternly.

Annoyed, he growled, "Woman! Call my name with respect."

"Argh!"

"Close the window and come and take the fish you wanted," Seigha sighed heavily. "We'll have to share it o."

"Come and see," she insisted.

Seigha hissed and continued eating.

"Peresuotei's house has gone into the sea," she mumbled and then began to murmur to herself. "Do you think that's where the singing has been coming from? Do you think the river people have come to complain again? I heard their song. Do you think they've returned to steal my soul after singing to me?"

Seigha shook his head, washed his hands, walked over to his wife's side to close the window and froze. He rubbed his eyes and grimaced from the sting of pepper. A little relieved from the sting, he peered out again, opening the window wider.

"Peresuotei's house is gone," Seigha said in a hushed whisper.

His wife turned to glare at him.

"Ebiye," he breathed, dread enveloping his heart. He hurried to the corner of the room to get his bell.

"What do you ned that for? Peresuotei will not be in his hut by this time."

"Ebiye," Seigha gestured and began to ring the bell.

"Who is Ebiye?" his wife asked, confused.

"His daughter. Peresuotei's daughter."

His wife laughed. She was still laughing as the men and their sons began to pour out of their houses; they assumed it was a quarrel, which was now common in the community. His wife's infectious laughter didn't help either.

Shaking his head, Seigha pointed to the spot that once had Peresuotei's house.

"Where is Peresuotei?"

"At the usual place," someone in the back mumbled.

Some men shrugged because they'd warned Peresuotei about fixing his house. Air bubbles spewed out, and the younger children looked on, fascinated.

"The girl with the singing voice," a little boy who'd been picking his runny nose and licking his phlegm said to a boy rubbing his stomach.

"Yes, it comes from there," an older girl mumbled.

"Maybe it's sea person," Seigha's wife offered.

"No. It's Ebiye, Peresuotei's daughter," Seigha insisted.

"No one even bears that name," Seigha's wife countered.

"It's not a common name, but someone does," an old man with white blotches on his head said, yawning and stretching. "She lives beside y-"

"That's what I've been trying to say," Seigha cried with relief and lowered his hand.

"Suala! Suoyo!" the old man called. Suala and Suoyo were the best swimmers in all the hamlets.

"They are still at sea," their mother answered from a house further down.

A dispute ensued among the onlookers. Whose child could swim under water? Why they should be vested in saving the girl? If the girl was in the water. While they debated, Timadi and Timieri, both orphans and outcasts, jumped into the water, swam towards the sunken house and dived in. After exclamations of horror and shock came the long, pulsing, tense silence as everyone had but given up on the boys when they bopped up with a plumpy girl between them.

As Seigha's house was the closest to the wreckage, which was now a poke of sticks from the water, they lifted her onto his awning. The shock of forgetting – not knowing for some - a fourteen-year-old was eroded by awe.

Ebiye struggled to breathe. She'd never learnt to swim. She felt pressure on her chest as the air in her lungs escaped in tiny bubbles to the water's surface just as she was going down tangled in her father's discarded fishing net.

As fear enveloped her, she struggled to get out of the net and failed, but she caught her sticks. She had almost slipped out of the net, but leaning forward to catch them further tangled her. By the time she'd stopped falling, it was dark all around her, but she noticed also that she wasn't struggling to breathe, so she inhaled sharply. It felt like she was suspended in the air as there was water around her, but not close enough to touch. She could see varied kinds of glowing fish and crustaceans in the water.

"Well, well, well, land dweller, you're very far from home," a deep, scratchy, watery voice spoke.

"Please help me," she murmured, glancing around to find the owner of the voice.

"Your relief is temporary. What do you need those sticks for?" an eerily calm voice suddenly echoed around her.

Startled, she looked around and firmly said, "Show yourself."

The voice cackled. "Do you think you can handle what you see?" the voice teased.

Shivers ran down her spine while she wondered what he meant.

"Hungry?" the voice asked.

She was about to shake her head, but her stomach rumbled.

"Why don't you stay with me in my watery world? You can always visit your fellow land dwellers whenever you want. You won't need to fish for fish."

A fish swam into her bubble and landed on the tangled net beside her before slipping down into the water beneath her.

She sneered; even if she could eat the fish, it was raw. Her mother had told her that river people were evil soul eaters. She knew that if they ate her soul, she'd never be able to join her mother in the afterlife. However, the movement of the raw fish gave her an idea.

She webbed some of the ropes from the fishing net around her sticks. She then tried to use one of them as a hook, but it didn't grasp onto anything except discolouring the water and chasing tiny animals around.

"Stop doing that this instant!" the voice commanded.

"I need to leave this place," she countered, her gaze fixed on the surface though she couldn't see it.

"Do you? No one has come in search of you. I can tell you have no one."

She frowned. Didn't she? She had a father who would be frantic when he returned. She was concerned about his safety too.

"Look up there. The canoes are still docked. No one has dived in search of you," the voice taunted.

She looked up, but it was too dark to see what he was talking about. She knew no one except her father and his best friend.

"Who are you?" she asked distractedly.

"Does it matter?" it asked in a soothing voice.

She crossed her arms, choosing to ignore the voice and its owner and focus on a way to get to the surface. It sounded upset when she struck the rock, so maybe it belonged to him or her; it had to be a him from its voice.

"Have you made up your mind?" the voice asked a long while later.

She blinked at the black mist appearing by the rock,

and she began to pull away.

"I could be like you," the voice said, morphing into a boy her age with rough hair and a weird smile on his face. "Or you could be me," it said and twirled into a female version of a half-fish, half-woman.

"I…" she stammered. "Not interested."

"Perhaps you'd be more willing as the air finishes. I'll give you some time to think."

She noticed that the bubble had reduced and was much closer.

"I'll not die here," she declared defiantly, though terrified.

"But you won't," the voice said.

She glanced around for its owner but couldn't find it. She began to panic again. It was more tolerable seeing its form as it was easier to tell where it was speaking from.

"Have you decided?"

She looked up warily. If only she could see up ahead; the sea was too big a place to go missing.

"Well, Immortal or not, I have no patience." He materialised into a man sinking. "So, sink," and then turned into a merman and gestured, "Swim."

She grimaced.

"I'll not swim your way."

"As you wish," it said, and the bubble disappeared, and she began to struggle to breathe. Her chest was on fire, so she began to clutch at it, praying for help as her eyes hurt like pepper had been poured into them.

She was losing her grip on life when she felt something tug her up on both sides.

Tension thickened with the increasingly anxious crowd.

"Is she alive?" someone had asked.

Seigha exchanged glances with his wife and nudged her. "Check her."

Seigha's wife shook her head and jumped, bumping into her husband when Ebiye began to cough.

"She's alive," someone from the house opposite exclaimed.

"Timadi! Timieri!" the young observers chanted until someone rang a bell from the other end of the village - Tubo, the village head, stumbled out of his hut after his wife rang the bell.

"What's happening here?" Tubo asked, still groggy from sleep.

One of his wives filled him in on the unfolding event. While his wife filled him in, some women had gotten into their canoes and crossed over to Seigha's house to look at the girl who had been tucked away for as long as she was alive.

Curious and concerned, Tubo asked for Seigha to offer his canoe as none of his were moored. Brooding, he alighted the canoe and climbed up the ladder to Seigha's awning. As he did, the crowd reluctantly patted.

Tubo swallowed as the women made Ebiye rise to her feet. She was dripping water, and her measly clothes clung to her body, revealing her gourd*like* shape tapered in endless legs. His throat clogged up when Ebiye brushed her wet nappy hair off her face to reveal large eyes, a tiny nose and pink, cherubic lips. Her skin glistened; it didn't have the wear and tear of salt water and sun.

"You are your mother's daughter," he whispered and blinked back tears; her mother had been his best friend, the love of his life, but she'd chosen Peresuotei to despise her father.

He lowered his gaze and swallowed again. Her nipples, like tiny seed buds, pointed at him from well-rounded breasts; her belly was flat, making the dip of her belly button obvious.

He slanted his head and closed his eyes: seeing Ebiye, the unrequited feelings he had for her mother were beginning to blossom, but he feared his first wife's wrath for his wife never made a promise she didn't keep.

"Papa, this is her, the one with the singing voice," his cousin's youngest son said. "I like her."

"You can't like her," a girl of the same age as the boy warned.

"Why not?" the boy asked with a frown.

"Because you like me, and she looks like mammy water."

Tubo remembered this same conversation with his first wife. They'd all been friends, and he'd bragged that he'd marry only one wife if he were to marry Ebiye's mother, but when asked to choose, she had chosen Peresuotei, who was an orphan at the time and was the only one who'd not brought family or *kaikai* to the *asking*.

Think with your head, not your heart, he urged himself and took a deep breath as he mused. *Peresuotei may have known that his debts would be called as soon as the men set eyes on his daughter; that's why he hid her.*

Trying not to gawk at the girl, he slanted his head

and lowered it so he was staring at the calm water near them. "What's your name, child?"

"Ebiye," she said, blinking up at him.

Tubo inhaled sharply. She had a gap in the middle of her upper teeth like her mother.

If he hadn't sworn to his first wife that he wouldn't marry another wife, he would have made Ebiye his fifteenth. She had a waist that could girdle healthy babies. He stealthily glanced around at the curious crowd and found not only the men leering at her but their sons also. It made him wish he had a son.

"Woman, why don't you take her in and clean her up?" Seigha, the only man not leering at her, said to his wife who glared at him so he added softly, "She can't remain here."

"She is even shivering," an old man said from his awning, which was inches away from Seigha's. "My house is big enough."

"No!" cried the men and boys.

"Why not?" Tubo's first wife, Nengi, asked, startling everyone; no one had heard her approach. She made a beeline to Tubo's side and saw a girl standing, wet from head to toe, her wet clothes clinging to her body, accentuating the curve of her breasts and hinting at the allure hidden beneath and sighed:

"Ah," Nengi sighed with a nod and frowned. "Why not? Abalagha is a good man. He has always been kind to our children."

The men's issue was deeper. Although Abalagha was a widower and partially blind in one eye due to a fishing accident, if Abalagha saw the girl properly, he might stake a claim, and if he did, he would be the most likely candidate to woo Ebiye.

"She would be in good company as he has a great

sense of humour," Nengi continued.

"No," Tubo said firmly. "She should stay with the women."

"I'm an honourable man," Abalagha protested from his awning.

"Yes," Seigha retorted. "You're a man regardless. The tradition still applies."

"Is it not tradition that has kept her away from her people?" Nengi cried. "We almost lost the poor girl."

Seigha nodded thoughtfully. "Why can't she stay with Ebikeme's daughters?"

"No," two boys cried out, and two of Ebikeme's daughters sighed with relief, surprising Tubo.

"She can stay with us," Timadi and Timieri offered.

Seigha smiled kindly at them as he said, "The tradition still applies to you. Thank you for saving Ebiye."

Tubo nodded in agreement. "*Nua.*"

"Well, she can't stay with the men, and most of the wives are afraid to let her in." Nengi subtly nudged Tubo and gestured for him to speak.

"In that case, I demand you offer up some of your daughters to stay with her, clothes, food and lamps. The rest of you go home and pray for Peresuotei's safe return."

Though Tubo lingered, averting his gaze was a struggle, but he could tell Nengi's eyes were schooled on him. Sighing, he halted and said:

"If you're a man, come to my house. If you're a husband or father, go home and settle your family before you join us."

To his surprise, when they climbed into the canoe to head home, Nengi took his hand in hers. Excitement fluttered in his belly, reminding him of how they used to be. She'd pushed him away for so long. Baffled, he pinched himself and glanced at their joined hands and her face.

"*Nua'o*," they greeted other passersby, and she didn't untangle her hand from his. He found he already missed her when she let go to climb the ladder. Some of the men were already heading in the direction of his house and he was willing to ignore them; it was going to be hard to get them to let Peresuotei's daughter go, he was struggling himself, but he was willing to fight the urge to go after her now that Nengi was giving him a chance.

As soon as he got to his awning, he pulled the bench out, contemplating a way to send Peresuotei's daughter out of the village. He was certain she would fall into a similar predicament, being constantly wooed after marriage, like her mother. He was still distracted when he felt a hand on his shoulder. He turned quickly, raising a questioning brow at Nengi.

Nengi stretched a hand toward him and said softly, "Come."

He obeyed and followed her to her section of his house, a place he'd been banned from for years. He was flushed with anticipation of crushing the barrier that had enveloped them for close to two decades; apprehension for all the unresolved issues that hung loosely in other sections of his house – the other wives; and a yearning for redemption for all the pain he'd caused her for his insatiable desire to outwit and outnumber every man in his community.

As Nengi drew the raffia curtain to give them privacy, he knew the test of his loyalty to her was going to be Peresuotei's daughter; he would need to take her out of the community, and the one person who could give him that opportunity and also cater to her needs was Abalagha.

He inhaled sharply when he turned around to find Nengi walking towards her mat, completely naked. Surprised at how quickly she had undressed, he fought the image of Ebiye's wet body and his rising desire, that he closed his eyes.

"Tubo," Nengi called, her voice tinged with impatience. She tapped the space beside her. She looked untouched by time.

"Nengi," Tubo stammered as he hurriedly took off his clothes. As he made his way to Nengi's side, he made a mental note to find a spouse for Peresuotei's daughter, a man who would take her away from Adonye-Ake.

Ebiye heard flitting, watery sounds along with a thumping sound. She was cold, wet and on a flat surface. She inhaled cautiously and found she could breathe normally. Amid chants of 'Timadi' and 'Timieri' were whispers: her father's voice was not among them. She burped, releasing water into her nostrils.

"She's alive," someone exclaimed.

Sneezing and coughing, she opened her eyes just as the people around her parted to let a man with a limp and hair as white as her father's come closer. She felt hands pull her up and frowned because they all smelt of stale fish.

"What's your name, child?" the man asked.

"Ebiye," she said, blinking to keep the seawater that had drenched her hair from entering her eyes.

She tried not to look around. She'd recognised some of the voices and wanted to attach faces to them, but it was difficult with the way they stared at her, especially after the man who had just joined them said:

"You are your mother's daughter."

She raised a brow when the man stealthily wiped a tear.

In the midst of the chants, the older people spoke about a place for her to stay, but none of them asked. It was almost like being in her father's house again. She'd been there long before her mother died and had had no guests. No one had cared, and now they were having a debate about her welfare.

The looks and the whispers from the women, then the men and the girls who were now with her, unsettled her. It reminded her of the vile thing.

Her unease deepened; there was profit and exploitation in every sentence, and she wondered what would happen if she had to live with any of these people. Looking for a distraction, she almost cried with relief when she found her sticks; they'd been knotted together with a fishing net, but there were still too many people between her and them. She suspected that the boys holding bits of coral in a different fishing net beside it had saved it.

As the skies darkened, the crowd dispersed, and soon four girls joined her on Seigha's awning. Timadi and Timieri offered two lamps which were different from the first one someone had brought; its wicker was thinner, its flame brighter, and it had no pungent smell of oil.

She made a mental note to thank Timadi and Timieri for saving her sticks. Somehow, she felt they were the only people she could relate with.

Feeling like a fish on display unsettled her so much that she was unable to sleep. She picked up the fishhooks Timadi must have forgotten and began to break and piece together the coral, making her sticks into one pole while yearning for her father to be alive, especially after three of the four girls whispered about leaving Adonye-Ake.

"I wish I had Da'Ebikeme's defiant spirit," one had said.

"I want to be like her," another girl said.

Contemplatively, she sat apart from the girls who'd also told her that Ebikeme was the only one who'd ever taken them seriously and even helped them sell their inventions secretly. She didn't need to be like Ebikeme; she was her. She'd fought for her life in the depths of the sea. Now, on the surface, she wanted more. She wasn't going to sink or swim. She just had to find a way to rise above the waters.

Ebiye glanced at the only other awning with lamps on at the other end of the village and sighed. She knew she was the topic of the men's discussion. Would she be nothing more than crayfish or periwinkle in the hands of those who sought to profit from her father?

She shook her head as ideas flitted through her thoughts while she continued knitting the coral to the wood, glad to have more than enough twine and string. She was just about to fall asleep when she heard:

"Ebiye! What are you doing there?"

Elated, she raised her head to see her father's face.

"Peresuotei," the man from before shouted from the awning at the other end of the village. "Come o! We've been waiting for you."

"Wait here. I'm coming," her father mouthed.

She nodded. When her father left, she heard one of the girls climb up to join them; she hadn't seen her leave.

"I went to bring pepper and fish. Do you want some?"

Ebiye shook her head. She was hungry, but she'd heard the man who'd just called her father tell them to not leave each other's side without a guardian.

Tubo sucked his teeth as he stared at the ripples created by the canoes faring the narrow passage between the houses, nodding to the greeting of the men coming to join him.

"My brothers, I see some of you about to keel over concerning Peresuotei's daughter, but you all have wives."

"We saw you too," Tubo's younger brother teased. "She looks like her mother."

Tubo nodded. "I've promised Nengi that there'll be no other."

Tubo smiled proudly as his brother's mouth hung open.

"My brothers, you can't all marry her... Ebiye. You each have several wives."

"Even you," one of them mumbled.

"I promised Nengi, 'no more wives'."

"Mmm," one of the men retorted in disbelief.

"We will deliberate when Peresuotei comes," Tubo said with finality moments later.

But none of them was patient, so while they deliberated, he wondered what would happen to his other wives or what Nengi would do if he were to take Ebiye as his fifteenth. He also kept an eye on Seigha's awning; he knew Peresuotei was sneaky and would have already been informed of his submerged house and the men's interest in his daughter and would want to sneak her out of the village, thereby causing an outrage.

It was morning when Peresuotei returned and was mooring an unfamiliar canoe near Seigha's house.

"Peresuotei," Tubo shouted out from his awning. "Come o! We've been waiting for you."

Peresuotei, still drunk, was worried and exhausted. As the canoe drew closer, he saw some of the men he owed and sighed in despair. He'd tried to keep his daughter away from the men in his clan, and now he'd left her exposed.

"You've given us a sleepless night. I thought you'd fallen into the water in a drunken stupor."

Peresuotei laughed nervously and climbed up to Tubo's awning.

"That's a beautiful daughter you have there," one of the men Peresuotei owed murmured as soon as Peresuotei joined them.

"*Serido*," Peresuotei greeted reluctantly.

"*Serido*," everyone else murmured.

"You want to – " Peresuotei swallowed and looked for Tubo.

"Yes, yes, yes," Tubo mumbled and grimaced when Peresuotei let out a strong burp, spreading the stench of stale alcohol. "We've been deliberating. All night about your daughter."

"I still insist that Abalagha is too old for her," one of the men mumbled.

Peresuotei frowned, confused, wondering what Abalagha had to do with the deliberations about his daughter.

"Sit down," Tubo ordered, but when no one offered him a space on the bench and stools. Tubo gave up his own for Peresuotei nudged one of the men to stand up for him.

"These men will forgive your debt if you let any of them marry your daughter," Tubo said, replacing the man who was now standing.

Peresuotei grimaced, recalling his promise to his late wife; their daughter was to marry among her peers, one who could give his life for her, a man who has no other wife.

"But they all have wives," Peresuotei chirped, averting his gaze as he was facing them on Tubo's stool. "More than one wife."

"That's why I suggested Abalagha. He is kind, and you don't owe him. I've been curious to know why he is the only one you're not owing."

Peresuotei removed his papa's cap and scratched his messy hair.

"How can you expect me to give her to a man who is closer to death than me," Peresuotei cried.

"My thoughts exactly," one of the men said, scratching his scrotum. "I'm the most viable candidate. I have only two wives and three children."

The other men began to argue amongst themselves while Peresuotei cradled his head in sorrow.

"Debt, like lust, is slow and easy, and its cravings deep," Tubo muttered to himself.

Peresuotei sighed, dipped his hand in his pocket and remembered that he'd used the last money he had for the sale of his last canoe to feed his habit.

"Peresuotei," another man started, "You have no house to keep your daughter. She has no chaperone.

You have no canoes. How do you hope to cater for her needs?"

Peresuotei grimaced, shifting uncomfortably, recalling Ebikeme had asked him these questions. He'd sold the canoe to buy the sticks that would have been used to fix the stilts.

"Tubo, your brother is right. Peresuotei, how do you hope to cater for her?"

Peresuotei hated these men's greed; like him, they lacked ambition except when it came to women and rearing children. He wished he had taken Ebikeme's offer.

"So, sink or swim, which will it be?" Tubo asked, sighing heavily and added, "Your daughter has a clean name, and she is a beauty. You know the flaws of these men, but if we can get Seigha's wife to chaperone her in the next big market day, then we'll only need to worry about her shelter until then."

Peresuotei's eyes widened with hope.

"We can't go to the market empty-handed," Tubo's brother pointed out.

"We should go further into the sea to make a decent catch this time."

"As you have no canoe, you'll have to go with one of us," another man said.

Tubo chuckled. "You'll go with me."

"What about Suala and Suoyo? They'd make a good candidate for marriage," Peresuotei said quickly. He didn't like either of them, and as they were brothers and unlikely to agree to anything except fishing, it could delay her getting married until she was a little older.

"They still live with their fathers, who are also interested in your daughter," Tubo gestured. "They are supposed to have their own houses according to –"

"Tradition," some of the men completed.

Tubo got up, signalling the end of the meeting. "Go and clean up. We must leave before the sun gets too hot. We will discuss this when we return."

Peresuotei was hungry, tired and worried. He'd run out of solutions because every solution he got he used it to buy *kaikai*.

"Those men are desperate," he sighed, and he took a deep breath and dipped himself in the cold water at the place designated for bathing, a few metres away from the houses. While he was there, he saw something glint in several shards. It was from the opposite side of where the sun faced. It was in the sea, and he was curious but not curious enough to go and check it out.

He wondered if it was something he could sell and pay off his debt. The more he stared at it, the more he wanted to investigate it, so he swam towards it when it got closer. It was a canoe, a rather large canoe.

"Peresuotei," Ebikeme mumbled.

He looked up to find Ebikeme looking down at him from the large canoe.

"*Serido*," Peresuotei greeted and looked around for a place to hold onto. "You're back."

"I am."

"What happened to your canoes? I can't reach –"

"Don't reach it," Ebikeme retorted, sounding irritated.

"You bought a bigger canoe," Peresuotei mumbled in surprise and licked his lips.

"What do you want?"

"I…" Peresuotei started and shook his head. She could be the help he needed, but he couldn't let her reach the village or it would foil his plan.

"Are the rumours true?" Peresuotei asked.

Ebikeme eyed him suspiciously.

"Are the monsters in the waters?"

Ebikeme crossed her arms and raised her head to glance at the village.

"I could get your daughters to come over to you so you won't need to enter the village," Peresuotei murmured and saw the glint of hope in her eyes but added, "Your second daughter may not want to follow you."

Ebikeme squinted at him.

"We've always been honest with each other."

Ebikeme nodded.

"She has been having a dalliance with Tarila." Peresuotei hesitated when he saw the pain in her eyes.

"Is she?"

"Nengi believes that she is, but it's quiet. I wouldn't have known if…"

"My daughter —"

"That's why you're here," she retorted, sniffed, and asked, "How is she?"

Peresuotei sighed heavily and, on a lighter note, asked, "How does someone get into this thing?"

Ebikeme stared at the village for a long time and sighed, untangled her arm and leaned forward. "You have to swim back."

Peresuotei was trying to figure out what to say when he noticed all four oars rise to beat the water and pulled back. Defeated, he watched Ebikeme's canoe move in giant strides as he swam behind it until he was close enough to head back to the bathing area.

He needed Ebikeme's help and would wait for her to greet her family before going to meet her again. He just hoped he could avoid the fishing trip with Tubo, or he'd lose the opportunity.

As he swam back, he wished he'd brought the money he'd made from selling his last canoe back to pay off one of the men he owed or at least used it to repair the stilts, and he wouldn't have exposed his daughter to the lecherous, greedy men of his community. His father-in-law was right; he was a good-for-nothing man. He'd made no effort to build on what his father-in-law had left his wife, thereby exposing his daughter.

Shaking his head to fight off his lightheadedness, he did a few laps before he passed out. He woke up to find himself on Tubo's canoe, scrambled into a sitting position and saw that Ebikeme's canoe was moored behind Seigha's house. He saw his daughter and a couple of girls around Ebikeme just as she looked in his direction, and he pointed at his daughter and nodded; he hoped Ebikeme understood what he meant. Ebiye would be better off with the one person who'd gone out of her way to care for his daughter without even leaving her house.

"You joined us today," Seigha said from his canoe. "Nua'o."

Tubo chuckled and slanted his head as he said, "Which hand would you have used to catch the fish if you were to use both to keep you above water?"

The men in the other canoes chuckled but had weird looks in their eyes. The type that told him he should have his wits about him, but he touched his pocket to find his bottle, but it was gone.

Ebiye observed the woman as the other girls who'd stayed with her circled her. Timadi and Timieri hovered from a distance. She wanted to thank the brothers for rescuing her, but there was so much noise that the woman had to hush them several times.

"You're your mother's daughter," the woman said solemnly.

Distracted by her thoughts, she lowered her gaze; there was a calmness in the woman's tone, almost soothing.

"Your mother was my best friend," the woman continued.

She frowned, not looking up, wondering why she never showed up when her mother was sick.

"She made me promise to keep an eye on you and to stay away from her when she was ill."

She looked up at the woman who had tears in her eyes.

The woman shrugged. "I used to be sick a lot, and she was worried she'd make it worse. Each time I tried to see her, she'd insist, 'I need someone to keep an eye on my daughter, and it's you'. It was the hardest thing I ever did."

She tried to hold back her tears and turned around to see the men at the other end of the village getting up. A few minutes later, she heard one of them let out a long whistle.

"It's the big market day today," one of the girls whispered excitedly.

"No, it's not. For us, at least," one of the women from last night said, climbing the ladder to join them.

"They're going fishing today."

"Fishing on a market day?" Timadi and Timieri asked in tandem.

"Where are your manners?" the woman scolded between panting when she got to the awning.

"Nua'o," they greeted.

"Why are you boys here?" the woman queried, turned around and gasped. She rubbed her eyes and asked in a tiny voice, "Ebikeme?"

"Nengi," the woman sighed, got up and wrapped her arms around the woman in a tight embrace.

"My sister, I've been worried about you," Nengi sighed.

"It went well, but I can't stay."

"You just got here," Nengi grumbled.

"I came to get my daughters," Ebikeme explained.

"I understand. I wish Peresuotei was here to give consent to take his daughter, too. She is in danger here."

Ebiye noticed that they shared a look, and Ebikeme gasped while Nengi nodded.

"I'll take her with me if she's willing," Ebikeme said, turning to her face.

A sense of foreboding washed over her as she looked at the woman. Everyone was a stranger, but there was a warmth with the woman.

"We must leave now," Ebikeme murmured.

Nengi looked downcast, cleared her throat, and smiled and then turned to her. "I agree."

"Ebiye, you must go with Ebikeme," Nengi inched closer and toucher her on the shoulder. "You'll go through what your mother went through if you stay."

"But my father," she started and turned to face the ocean. Several canoes were heading out to sea. They'd gone a long distance, but she could make out her father; he was sleeping. He'd told her to wait.

"There's nothing he can do for you now. You'll be safer with Ebikeme," Nengi insisted.

"Can we come along?" Timadi and Timieri asked, inching closer.

"Are you sure?" Ebikeme asked them, looking concerned. "If you follow me, you can't return."

"I don't want to go with you," the girl who had left and returned with food said quickly.

"Understandably," Ebikeme and Nengi replied in unison.

"There's nothing for us here," Timieri said.

Timadi nodded in agreement.

"You said it went well," Nengi interjected, eyeing Ebikeme suspiciously.

"It went well, but the waters between is not kind," Ebikeme sighed heavily. "The ground is fertile but untilled."

"You've got your work cut out for you," Nengi acknowledged, sweeping her gaze over the others. "But these are the best kids, and I know they'll prosper with you."

She watched the dissenting girl descend the ladder and glanced back at Ebikeme. Ebikeme was blinking back tears while the boys looked on eagerly. She frowned at what they'd said about having nothing to keep them here. They had gone out of their way to help, even saving her sticks. If she didn't have them, she would still be okay because she had her father albeit almost always absent. She was a little disappointed as she would have liked to get to know them.

Deciding to wait for her father, she picked up her now bejewelled stick and the remaining corals and stepped back from the others. Hopeful, she turned to face the endless water just as her father bolted upright, pointing in her direction and nodding. She suspected he was telling her to go with Ebikeme.

Obliging him, she turned to face Ebikeme, who'd just turned away from everyone to wipe her tears. Embarrassed, she turned away, biting her lip to hold back hers.

She climbed down from Seigha's hut right after Ebikeme's daughter, Tubo's nieces, and another girl who'd seen Ebikeme and came with all her things, Timadi and Timieri, followed her after Ebikeme. It was quiet in the canoe until someone gasped when they got to the back of Seigha's house, where Ebikeme had moored her oversized canoe.

Ebikeme skilfully pulled a big string with knots, which they used to climb into the canoe. In the canoe, she watched Ebikeme undo the twines of the fishing nets that had secured all the oars, so that they moved in tandem when one oar moved.

Overwhelmed with trepidation and in resignation to her new fate, she turned her back to the sounds of awe as the others smoothed their hands on the surface of the polished wood, asking Ebikeme questions and comparing notes. The mass of fishermen heading out to sea had long disappeared. She exhaled heavily, swiping the tears that reached her cheek, hugged her cherished stick, and watched the only place she'd called home fade into the meeting of sky and sea in the distance.

AGNES KAY-E, a Nigerian residing in England, with a portfolio of twelve books spanning multiple genres. Among her notable works is the bestselling novel Blossom in Winter. Her latest release, Cursed Blossoms, delves into African magic realism, showcasing her versatility as a writer.

Beyond her literary pursuits, she finds solace in singing and composing music during her spare moments.

Additionally, she has been actively engaging with readers through a live book chat channel on Instagram every Saturday since October 2021, featuring over 200 authors to date.

AJEJI

– Aisha Oredola

Abike smiled before slipping the copper bracelet on her wrist, the kind that hid secrets and made men humiliatingly weak in her presence as it stretched her lips in a way that lit her face, reflecting her beauty. It had an ethereal effect on souls, calming their troubled minds. Many wanted to demystify her, but Odejimi loved her, the darkness and the light that came with her existence.

It was dangerous to meet her at midnight, defying orders from his brother, to speak with her alone, not knowing the type of blood that ran through her veins, not knowing where her people migrated or originated from. He did not care. The feeling of calm that embraced him whole when he settled his eyes on her face was like that of the night's moon glow in the wideness of the merciless dark sky. She was not another stray antelope he hungrily wanted to prey on, using his desires as sharp as canines soullessly with the same dexterity in his use of a spear. Abike was sacred, like a prayer sent to the heavens. Abike, the igniter and tamer of his wild lusts and straying mind. The gods know he used to chase any woman for the brief pleasure she could offer, which he snatched as he willed. Abike had shown him that a man could be genuinely smitten by a woman, totally whipped by her soul.

"This is too much, and you know it."

"Is it?" Odejimi let out a panicked sigh. "It's nothing really. You are worth it and more. I got it from Oja-Oba, close to Afin. Do you like it?"

She half circled her wrist in a swift arc, raising the bracelet to catch the light from the moon. It glowed against her brown skin, belonging there in a way that made Odejimi swear in his head that he wouldn't take it back, even if she insisted.

"This is dangerous." Abike's bottom lip hit the tip of her tongue as she pursed her lips, passing a message that Odejimi understood too well and frighteningly so. "It's beautiful. I like it, but my father…"

"Abike…" He inched closer, closing his hands on hers.

"What are we doing?" she asked, then repeated Odewole's words. "I come from a long line of unknown, lost, and probably cursed souls, remember? A nameless, wicked clan. A generation of aliens, strange foreign beings." Those were the string of words Odewole, his brother, had used on her nights ago when he caught them chatting and laughing under the

Kapok tree near her family's hut; he had followed Odejimi's closely.

"I'm sorry about Odewole," Odejimi muttered under his breath. *He has no warmth.*

Abike saw the anger flash in Odejimi's eyes at the mention of what his brother had said. It gave her this ecstatic child-like excitement that he cared for her and would defend and choose her over his brother if it came to it. Their relationship had reached that level where she was certain he would do anything to keep what they had. Abike smirked and then made a sad face almost immediately to garner more sympathy from her lover. "Is it only Odewole you're sorry about? Or your entire family?" Abike crouched down to pack a handful of sand. Her coral anklet jingled, drawing his eyes to the beads from the string. "Because they all hate me."

"Forget them." His tone was desperate. She had to stop bringing his family up. What they thought of her was their ordeal. He remembered when she went to the stream for a swim and to get some water, how some men had lurked behind the trees waiting for her to undress and have her bath while they stole glances at what was not theirs. He knew of them because he had overheard their plans to peep at the marketplace the last market day when they were unsuspecting, against the noise of buyers and sellers doing some trade by barter. The mention of her name alerted him when it came out of unworthy mouths. That morning, at dawn, Odejimi had gone ahead of her, knowing the time she usually came to the stream, hiding in the bushes. At the sound and sight of these lustful men, men he used to be like, he lunged at them, threatening them with his spear. They fled like shameless cowards.

"Odejimi?" Abike called in fear. "Is that you,

Odejimi?'

"Yes, my love. Everything is fine now."

He embraced her, dipped her water gourd in the stream and waited for her. When she was done with her swim, he carried her gourd to her family hut. The long walk was worth it all. They had talked, laughed, and shared future fantasies. At the door of her family hut, she thanked him for protecting her.

All this, and he could not give up spending time with her just because of his family's disapproval. "You really should forget them."

"They're right, actually. I'm bad for you."

"Don't say that." Odejimi sighed, drenched in anxious sweat. "I want to be with you, in life and in death." He placed his arms on her shoulders.

She talked on, not stopping to reply to him. "My blood. My nature. My dark side." Her fingers released the sand grains. His eyes followed their fall before his palm found hers. His hand was twice the size of hers.

"I only see light."

Abike scoffed. He had no idea what he was saying. Her dark side was cold and emotionless. She did however she pleased, working alongside her father to bring justice to earth however brutal their treatment of certain souls got in the underworld. He did not understand. He would soon understand.

"You said earlier that you want to be with me in life and in death? Like you know what it means," she uttered mischievously.

Abike raised her head to the heavens. The pagoda-shaped crown of the gigantic tree held the intensity in her eyes. The tree branches had many leaves that seemed like canopies for their tiny figures. They were shifting in patterns that turned Odejimi's eyes, so he looked at Abike's face for stability. That was when he tripped, landing on his right hip. It felt like an enemy was driving the blade of a sharp cutlass into his pelvic bone. Odejimi groaned in excruciating pain, stumbling and falling to the dry ground every time he tried to get up.

"I almost lost myself, you see? You're quite attractive, and you seem to be obsessed with me. It's intoxicating, your obsession."

As he struggled, Abike's words grew stranger. The look on her face stung his eyes. She was causing him so much pain that he felt twisted from the inside. Above them, the deciduous tree was shedding all of its leaves. They littered the ground ceremoniously, covering fine sand. Odejimi tried to stand again. His legs failed him. Abike's slow walk around his struggling body trapped his words, and he couldn't speak them even when he opened his mouth. Only groans escaped them. He was a voiceless, helpless cripple.

"You may have love to give to me." She gestured dramatically with a fallen branch in her hands. "Even with all the glass hearts you've shattered for the quest of their flesh." She stroked the bracelet, shaking her head. "A hunter's instincts indeed." The coral beads around her neck bounced victoriously as she pranced around him. "I would've given you another chance, but I was only assigned to you, and the assignment is always superior."

The wind blew in her direction, raising her chunky braids and, eventually, her feet. Odejimi groaned louder. The pain was unbearable. His vision blurred as the earth slowly split beneath his frame, driving him to unconsciousness.

"I'm taking you to my world now."

It was the eighteenth century. The year 1725. A time when Oyo-Ile of the Oyo Empire was at its most powerful and expanding to its finest state, especially with the trading with European merchants on the coast through the port of Ajase. Oyo's wealth increased exponentially, and they focused on amassing more wealth for territorial expansion, but with wealth came greed, which was also a period of ruthlessness. Its people were too vain, ravaging the lands. Robbing one another of valuables and property, taking women in many numbers for wives and several more as concubines, only to maltreat them, drinking to foolishness and ruling in the worst of ways.

It was not that people did not already have the compass for going astray, but the creatures of the other world became untethered, intensifying the chaos. Many of them encouraged madness, which only led them astray. Spirits, animals, beasts and foreign kinds took human forms to lure the blind into pits where their souls were the prize. The idea was to fill their heads with vanity, making them waste time while time wasted their lifespan. It was a dance to death.

These creatures would seize every opportunity to lure men into darkness, make them forget their creator, fill their loins with desire and sin, saturate every thought of theirs with insatiability and a never-ending quest for power and then punish them for their weaknesses. In this period, where whatever was supposed to be sacred was tainted and insulted, death and disappearance worked together mercilessly. Time was their companion, working in sync, snatching souls when it was due, their bodies occupying graves and the afterlife revealing itself to them, unknowing to many.

In this mess of the collision of two worlds, the Ajeji

found their way into Oyo-Ile and its neighbouring towns. Abike's people, a family of three generations, were assigned to Oyo-Ile, loathed by the intelligent townsmen because of their strange ways, flawless appearance and extraterrestrial nature. They all wore coral beads and brass jewellery like royalty from the Kingdom of Dahomey but claimed to be a family of Chiefs. Many loathed them for their vagueness. Others were merely baits weakened by their misleading appearance.

"Beware of people that look too good to be true." Odewole had told Odejimi one day when they were hunting for antelopes in the thick forest greens. He was afraid for his brother's safety. These people looked too important to just come from the Kingdom of Dahomey. There were several theories about their origin, and the one most people stuck with was that they were castaways from a strange land, castaways who pretended to be from the Kingdom of Dahomey.

The story they told the Alaafin of Oyo about being a family of Chiefs that were not appreciated in Dahomey and decided to seek refuge in Oyo-Ile before he granted them permission to stay was partially believable, especially because they were a family of many talents and proved themselves within the timeframe of observation set by the Oba and his chiefs. They even swore to help the Oyo Empire completely conquer and subjugate the Kingdom of Dahomey, but all these did not move Odewole and his family like many others.

"Even if they are from the Kingdom of Dahomey, which I strongly refuse to believe, they must be spies and will be the beginning of the end of the Oyo empire."

Odejimi said nothing.

Odewole pressed on. "Do you think a tribute-paying state to the Oyo Empire won't come for revenge? They probably want to expand and throw us off."

"You're too paranoid."

Odewole was about to speak when Odejimi placed his palm over his mouth and whispered. "Do not make a noise." He picked up his spear. "That's our meat."

"You have brought another one."

Abike flashed a content smile. "Did you doubt me, father?"

The Ajeji man paused, lifting his shoulders slightly. "Yes," he admitted, digging his fingers into his beard. "I was afraid the hunter would trap you, my darling."

"He almost did father." Abike flashed the bracelet across her face, her smile sinister.

They carried on, their voices rising and falling against the backdrop of hundreds of cries and screams.

"But the assignment is always superior," Father and daughter chorused finally.

Smoke replaced Abike's physical self; it filled the height of her stance before clearing like no one was even there. Kilani, Abike's father, motioned to some guards before stomping his staff on the muddy ground and disappearing into nothingness.

Odejimi, now conscious, opened his eyes to the nightmare of his new reality. His limbs were chained, and the cold of the bare ground travelled to his body through the soles of his feet, causing him to shiver. He scanned his environment and saw that he was with so many tattered and battered-looking people. As the memory of what he recalled last hit him, his voice came back.

"Abike? Abike! Where am I? Get me out of here!"

The others around him looked faded and worn out, a shadow of life, a semblance to misery. His sore throat burned as he screamed weakly, coughing terribly in the end.

A man who could carry his chains well looked at him with heavy pity.

"Stop yelling. It's a waste," the man said dryly, turning to his left.

Odejimi examined the man's face. It was weary, and the skin was dusty and had scars. He wondered how long he had been here.

"Anyone who is here is the reason for their own doom."

Odejimi ignored the man.

"Please! Let me out!" he shouted until his voice cracked, and he started breathing rapidly. The tears fell from his eyes slowly, wetting his dark skin and making it slippery. He yelled and wept for hours on end, burning what little energy left in him until hours later when he gave in to the seduction of sleep.

The next day came, but it was the same in the land of Ajeji. There was no way to tell if it was night or day. The shifting and dragging of feet tied in chains alone was depressing. Odejimi blinked back hot tears at his unexpected misfortune. He was sniffing loudly when the man next to him sighed.

"You can't possibly still be crying?"

Odejimi ignored the man and rose with lethargy from the dusty floor of the massive pit. His elbows and knees were white in contrast to his dark skin. "Who did I offend? Ehn? What have I done?"

His whimpering and self-pity annoyed the man. "All that is fruitless here."

"Leave me alone, please."

The way he bellowed pushed the man to a sinister laugh.

"What's so funny?" Odejimi, full of rage, asked

"You can't be left alone here. Or can't you see?"

For the first time since Odejimi was thrown into the dungeon pit, he scanned every corner carefully. Men and women alike, soiled in dirt, looking pitiful and hungry. Their bodies lean and malnourished.

"How many are we?" He asked, shivering and shaking. Shaking and shivering.

"How will I know?" The man shrugged. "Of what use is that to me?"

"You'd rather be so passive?"

The man coughed and spat some phlegm to his left. "Ehen? Will shouting and counting bring me freedom?"

"There are probably over a hundred of us on this site. One of many," whispered an old man seated cross-legged behind them. "Nobody lasts here," he hissed. "Many perish daily."

"What did we do? Why are we here?" Odejimi snapped impatiently, trying to free himself from the chains to no avail.

"Different reasons for each prisoner," the old man smiled wryly. "Soon you'll find out."

"Agba," Odejimi sighed. "How long have you been here?"

"I don't know young man," he replied. "But hundreds have perished before me."

"And why haven't you?"

"My punishment is different."

Odejimi dragged his feet up, searching for what he did not lose, shouting obscenities to whoever was in control.

"Please save your strength for tomorrow," the first man, Akin, said, bored with Odejimi's display.

"And what is tomorrow?"

"Mind travel test."

Odejimi buried his face in his chained hands. All he did was love a strange woman.

Crows were flying about, pounding ears with loud, repetitive caws and irritating coos. The noise increased with every complaint the prisoners made. Odejimi pressed his hands against his ears, but the sound penetrated them. He shut his eyes to find some calm, and surprisingly, it worked. When he opened it, he was alone, with no chains restricting his limbs. At first, he worried about the location of the others and why he was alone, then he froze. With nothing holding him down, he set to run. Surrounding him in an instant were spinning forest trees boxing him in. Odejimi tripped with dizzy eyes. He did not know he was fighting for air when he turned twice, searching for an exit.

That was when he saw her. She was staring directly at him with hateful eyes and an infant in her cradled arms, nursing on her bosom. Odejimi blinked a couple of times as if to blink her away. It was a waste. Ewatomi stood there unfazed. As she took steps towards him, he moved backwards, waving his hands remorsefully in front of his face.

"Please. Ewa, please."

Terrible cries erupted from the infant in a way that brought Odejimi to his knees. When Ewatomi was inches close, he shivered, covering his face with his hands. "You're dead. You're dead."

"Murderer!"

"Please go away," he whimpered, bowing his head between his shaky legs.

There was a wicked laughter above him, different from the cries but worse. When he dared to look up, the baby vanished, and Ewa's face morphed into another woman's. Odejimi found himself squinting to recognize her.

"The great hunter who finally got caught."

"Motolani?" Odejimi quaked in a croaky voice.

He did not notice the swell in her belly before. When he did, it faded, and she became another woman: plumper this time, a lighter shade of skin, a head-turning attractive lady. Royal beads graced her neck and waist. She smiled.

"Princess Labake."

"Odejimi." A horsetail whisk was in her right hand. She raised it when he started to blabber. "You deserve to be ruined by the Ajeji. You deserve for your life to be in turmoil the way you've messed with the lives of others."

With tear-filled eyes blurring his sight, he pleaded, placed his hands together like for a prayer and begged. "I'm so sorry."

Abike appeared before him with his next blink. She was unsmiling and angry, her eyes reddening with every breath she took, darkening the slowly growing atmosphere. Odejimi froze. The pain he felt under the Kapok tree returned twice as much.

"You're not sorry, you liar."

"Abike, stop! Enough with the mind games!"

"And that arrogance is proof." She smirked, raising her hands to the heavens. When she brought it down, Odejimi found himself back in the pit with the other prisoners. He did not know if relief was what he felt or intense confusion mixed with fear.

"Have you figured it out yet?" the old man asked a worn-out Odejimi, who responded with an empty stare, the evidence of being forlorn and drained of every light the world had to offer.

"The mind travel test has wrecked him, Agba," Akin sighed. "Like it did to us all."

"Young man." The old man faced Odejimi. "You're paying for your actions, and the Ajeji are dealing with you for sure."

"The Ajeji." Odejimi scoffed. Abike seemed pretty normal-looking to him... except for her mystical powers and supernatural abilities. How could he not see it? This woman he was ready to drop his casanova ways for was not even normal but a spirit Dahomey woman in human form ready to make the rest of his life meaningless and leave him trapped in a world of darkness with other lost souls. He never even touched her. He planned to settle down with her and do things the right way. He never saw her as a tool to be used. He loved her.

If he was being truthful to himself, he deserved this. Treating women less than animals was his crime. He preyed on them until he was done. Chewed their meat and cracked their bones before spitting out what was left of it. Those three women were just representatives of all the others he had torn apart with lies, deceit, anything to part their legs and grind his desires away.

Ewatomi had carried his child. She had come to him in the crack of day with a face swollen from overnight crying and ankles swelling with the symptoms of pregnancy, mumbling and jumbling words. He did not let her in. She stood at the entrance of the mud house, explaining with nervousness how he was the first man to lay with her and, in the process, got her pregnant. Odejimi chuckled, ridiculing her presence, and he saw the shame reflect on her face.

Denying was the least of his crimes. He called her names and dragged her away from his compound like an animal dragged to be slaughtered. Months later, her bump was obvious, and the people labelled her with dirty tags. On her due date for labour, she struggled for hours on end until her strength could no longer aid her, and she breathed her last; neither mother nor child survived. Odejimi did not shrug.

Motolani and Princess Labake's cases were similar. He led them on and took advantage of them. They used to be best friends, and he made sure that was history.

But was Motolani pregnant?

"You're figuring things out?"

When he raised his head to see the speaker, he saw that he was alone again with Abike.

"Abike, please. I don't know what else to say or do, but please, I'm extremely sorry for everything." He was sorry. His treatment of those women was because he did not know what love was. His thoughts were consumed with the flames of lust, and ruthlessly, he took from the honey pots of women who trusted him with their hearts. Abike was the first woman he ever truly fell carelessly for. It turns out that love picked the wrong time.

"Quiet! You have no shame." Her braids were

turning into smoke from their roots atop her head. "Let me explain this thing to you."

Knowing better was supposed to be an option for Odejimi. Adversity, however, has its ways of surprising a person over and over. The explanation was not something of words alone. Next to Abike appeared a man clad in a guard's uniform made from a tiger's skin. A sheath hung loosely from his side, bearing a sword, but he knew the guard did not rely on that weapon. He must've extraterrestrial abilities of his own. Just when Odejimi thought it was over, more guards appeared. He counted. About six of them stood protecting an already impenetrable spirit alien woman. *Ajeji Obinrin.*

"Daily, we capture souls who have erred exponentially in the land of the living. Especially those who try to deceive the Ajeji." More parts of her turned into smoke. Like her feet and hands. "You tried to deceive me, Odejimi, son of Odelabi. Luring me into a marriage where you would finally get in between my thighs, right? In the guise of love."

"No! That's not true, Abike. I loved you."

"Silence!" The lead guard said, bringing down a whip with spikes on Odejimi's back. He bled profusely, wincing at the pain, red blood soaking through his ragged Buba.

"Men are too predictable." She summoned the gold bracelet, which ended up in her smoke-like hands. "After what you did to all those women, or should I say victims. Ajeji decided to test you, and you failed."

"Please, please, I beg of you…"

The whip hit him harder, drawing more blood.

"SHUT UP!" the guard bellowed.

"They never learn." Abike grinned evilly.

Odejimi knew not to say a word.

"I read minds." She crouched down to his eye level. "Your love was half true, and I only do full."

Odejimi shook his head. He loved her fully. He swore he did. He started panting heavily when the guards seized him by his limbs. Shouting for help did him no good, as he got whipped anytime he did. Abike led the guards. The closer they got to their destination, the more screams and cries grew louder. When they reached the spot, she turned to face them.

"This is the end."

Once her back was turned, the guards threw Odejimi into the underground cage with the starved lion. His fall was slow, with his life flashing before his eyes. He loved Abike. He loved her. He did not deserve an end like this. Love was supposed to be merciful to him, kind even. He had made himself a marionette for his lover, Abike, the puppeteer. Only for his life to be toyed with, like its strings were insignificant. Love was supposed to be forgiving, not a tool of destruction, when the weakness of your lover is in the palm of your hands. Love had played him. He, who struck beasts of the forest with his spear, was now in the position of his prey. Who gave these strange spirits, these aliens, the right to wrap up people's lives? His thoughts followed him into the mouth of the beast.

"Dust upon dust."

That voice.

Abike raised her head to the heavens. The pagoda-shaped crown of the gigantic tree held the intensity in her eyes. The tree branches had many leaves that seemed like canopies for their tiny figures. They were shifting in patterns that turned Odejimi's eyes, so he looked at Abike's face for stability. That was when he tripped, landing on his right hip. It felt like an enemy was driving the blade of a sharp cutlass into his hip. Odejimi groaned in excruciating pain, stumbling and falling to the dry ground every time he tried to get up.

"We will all turn into dust, you know?"

Odejimi rubbed his eyes vigorously. What was happening to him? Did he travel back in time, or was all he experienced some sort of futuristic event that he could still prevent now? He looked at Abike, and she grinned evilly, walking around him.

"No," he whimpered. "Please go away. Stay away from me." When he tried to get up this time, he did so effortlessly and began to run as fast as his legs could carry him.

Abike found amusement in his act. Laughed wickedly and knowingly. She had taken him to the world of Ajeji and brought him back because he really did love her, but it was best to teach him a lesson. He should consider himself lucky. Not everyone came out of the Ajeji world alive, especially those who laid in bed with Ajeji women or men. Those ones had already made blood covenants with them.

Abike did try to seduce Odejimi several times. He refused, claiming he wanted to do things right. He was lucky. Very lucky. The sacred was kept sacred.

Abike tapped her feet thrice on the ground, sending vibrations to wherever Odejimi's feet were placed in the town. The vibrations passed through him, and this took effect immediately. He would never be able to reveal the secrets of the Ajeji to another, even if he tried to. The memories of his experience will be his alone to deal with. And the Ajeji would not leave Oyo-Ile yet. The punishment of these humans had only begun. Let them merry and stray away, disrespecting what is sacred and trading their souls for mere low desires. The Ajeji world awaits.

AISHA OREDOLA, a scholar with a background in public health and genetics, defies expectations by immersing herself in the world of literature. Her passion for writing spans fiction and non-fiction genres, earning recognition in esteemed publications like Brittle Paper, NTBF Anthology, and Blue Minaret Literary Journal. Aisha's accolades include winning the Panacea Essay and Short Story Writing Contest and earning a spot on the Collins Elesiro Prize long list.
Her debut novel, Rid Me of This, promises captivating narratives that showcase her diverse talents and dedication to storytelling.

HOW KINGS ARE MADE

- *Jesimiel Williams*

The broken Anglican church looms in the village centre, a skeletal monument casting long shadows that smothered the land. An endless blanket of clouds hides the moon, and the quiet of the night mirrors the emptiness of the night sky and the hundreds of darker and empty worlds that shroud it behind clouds and stars.

The night is thick with an unsettling quiet. The broken Anglican church stands in the centre of the village like a skeletal monument, its shadows smothering the land, the moon hidden by an endless blanket of clouds.

Whenever the moon goes missing, the village holds its breath as though it is one of their kinsmen who has taken a trip, and whether he'll return remains unsure. As such, moonless nights are not for the living to roam, and even the naked little boy, who often streaks across the village with his grandmother in chase, is tucked away in his hut.

It's a time when the wind carries whispers of women who meld with black cats and bats so that their shadows dance with malevolent grace, and they cross the boundaries between human lands and where the *Orisha* lay their head. The very air tastes of bile and uncertainty at the thought that you may step out to pee in the bush and disturb a coven of cats, attracting an unliftable curse.

When the summons from the village came for Tunde, our minds were far from any expectations of a malevolent and moonless night. Lagos was too noisy for such.

When Daddy's phone rang, it remained untouched for a minute, everyone postponing the duty to call my father to his dancing plastic box.

When he answered the phone finally, anyone could tell it was not one of the calls that asked when we would be sending daddy's driver to Ifo to collect the corn at the farm or to complain about the poor harvest that the grazing herders had made worse. Those started with mock greetings and laughter between my father and his, in pretence of the fact that they rarely got along.

Daddy had hidden himself in the corner of the living room to take the call, away from mummy's fraying prayer mat in the corner of the room and closer to the ugly totem pole that was our book stand, whispering in tiny sprints of seeming gibberish. Short whispers were always a sign in our home that something was wrong. Perhaps the gas cylinder had emptied, and there wasn't a dime to spare to refill it, or Tunde's girlfriend was pregnant, and her father wouldn't stop calling our mother, threatening hell on earth.

When Tunde had gotten Layo pregnant, my mother had screeched in our living room as though she had been hit by a car or a trailer, better still, Tunde remained on his knees mumbling what sounded like apologies, and Layo sobbed and apologized loudly until her nose ran like the stream you could see from our kitchen window. But what apology would take the child back to heaven where it came from?

Father, we're sorry. We didn't mean to have a baby yet? Please take him back, and it won't happen again.

Mummy would calm down as much as was humanly possible for her. Sitting and knocking her knees against each other, mumbling to herself about Sunday School and other less audible things. Eventually, she invited Pastor Joju to speak to 'her son and his fiancée' and begin counselling them for a wedding, whether they wanted one or not. My Father wasn't in support of a wedding. Weddings are expensive, he had said. My mother and Pastor Joju disagreed vehemently. They insisted that God would provide for the wedding.

Pastor Joju had eyebrows that were double mine and bushier than a chicken's tail, both of which constantly flared up whenever he visited us and preached about the dangers of hell while glancing at my father from the corner of his eyes. My father had told us after the pastor's first visit that only women paid attention to men like him, and he wouldn't eat without them.

Several months later, when Layo went missing before the wedding – and we would find out she later had gone to the north to marry a reverend she met on Facebook, Pastor Joju would subject Tunde and my mother to bouts of prayer and fasting to 'bring back our possessed wife'. It was the first time I said out loud that it was either God didn't answer the prayers Pastor Joju prayed, or he had just answered Tunde's secret prayers to save him from early marriage instead. My father had laughed out and nodded in assent.

It was Pastor Joju who came to mind as my father turned his back to take the phone call. I could just see the pastor's greying eyebrows and the scowl they would take upon hearing that there was another wedding to be planned and a couple to be counselled.

I looked at my brother Tunde; he was seated with his back to the wall, and the poor lighting made him appear hunchbacked. His face was without expression and lacked the tinge of worry I knew to be present whenever he had baked himself a violent loaf of catastrophe. This call wasn't about him, was it?

Who is pregnant this time? Grandpa's seventeen-year-old wife?

I would find that no one was having a child this time, no person anyway. The days that would follow, however, were pregnant with dark foreboding for me. Perhaps it was our hurried trip at twilight to the bus park in Agege, where my father seemed pressed to ensure that no one saw us board the rickety bus as though our lives depended on it.

The journey from Lagos to the village near Ifo was always a long one. Not because it was a great distance but because the road would deteriorate the further along we got. If you had thought it was a good idea to buy a bowl of soup when the bus pulled out of the park, you would find that it would end up all over your clothes halfway through the journey.

The government would make promises to begin

repairs on the road during every election cycle, but like the weather report from the morning, they couldn't be counted on. Dark clouds already loomed over the village ahead of us, and it seemed to be the sign that we had crossed from the point where it mattered if you had a driver's license or your seatbelt was on, now on to largely ungoverned lands.

Mama Ibeji, our grandmother, was the first one to welcome us as we crested the hill after alighting from the creaking bus over to where our small village marked its spot in a clearing. In a faded shirt that once had a church logo and the text 'Let's go fishing', the old woman enveloped me and Tunde in a large hug. She smelled like corn and fermenting cassava, just like the last time.

"Bawo ni, Nibo ni iya rẹ wa?" she asked if our mother had come with us.

Daddy shook his head, and his eyes seemed to speak to his mother, an understanding passing between them. The messages passed from mothers to their children with simple glances remain our culture's Morse code, simple yet encrypted.

Mummy hated making trips to the village. She claimed that demons lived here and could hide in your bags and return to the city with you following a visit. It was standard practice to leave our bags on the floor outside the apartment doors until Mummy had sprinkled them with some of the anointing oil that Pastor Joju had sold us, and only that seemed strong enough to return the demons home and away from our belongings. It bothered me that the demons of the city couldn't come home to the village in our bags, too, the ones that made people rush into the metal buckets we called buses at 5 am.

The clouds are hidden from our sight when we sit in one of Baba Ibeji's huts, the roofing shielding us from whatever the sky has in store next. We sat, I cross-legged, and Tunde, with his legs stretched out in front of him, on our grandfather's raffia mat. My grandfather and Father were seated across from each other, and short glances passed between them as they ate. The raffia mats were centred with plastic bowls and clay bowls, all in white and brown. The vegetable soup was a mixture of leaves foreign to me, and the palm oil that would usually host a myriad of floating condiments seemed like an open and unfettered sea instead. Something has changed here.

"The gods have chosen your brother, you know?" Baba Ibeji said abruptly in Yoruba. He looked me in the eye and seemed to burrow into me for an answer to a question I knew nothing of. His old eyes were now dimming grey, making me wonder if he could see me.

"Chosen him for what?" I asked, and the ensuing silence appeared to render my question foolish. My father soon spoke up quickly in Yoruba, a rush of words that sounded like an excuse, seeking to please his king of a father. "I haven't told Leye yet."

"I thought so," Baba Ibeji answered in kind. Whenever my father and his father sat together to speak, the air seemed to thicken with an unspoken divide between them both. I knew nothing of what had splintered their relationship, but it was clear to anyone that my grandfather regarded my father just a little above his hunting dogs.

Baba Ibeji turned to me, the animosity he bore my father dissipating like the vapour above a steaming teacup. "Your brother is going to become Oba."

I turned to look at Tunde. Our eyes met briefly, and

he nodded in agreement. He never had much to say recently, and this was no exception. His oily forehead glowed with pride in the low light of the mud-walled room. He didn't look like a king to me.

But what does Tunde know about being a king? Not any more than me or anyone we know.

The question bore on my mind until I was sure I had worried a hole into my brain where my concerns about my brother could pour in. I did that often, thinking and bothering about things I had little to no control over. It never made me any more prepared when it happened, but it convinced me I was a little intuitive or clairvoyant.

"Why Tunde?" I blurted, and all eyes turned to me at once. I immediately wished I had instead upturned my bowl of soup onto the raffia mat and begun to chew on the clay that made up the walls. Baba Ibeji turned to face my father and brother as though saying, *'Look at the boy'*.

"Awọn orișa ti pașẹ rẹ," he answered. "It's what the orisa has said, that the son of my son will be king."

That's barely a prediction. If you died and your son died, Tunde would be king either way.

"I understand," I lied. I didn't believe in the traditional gods, the ones that were wood and ate boiled eggs and yams. What kind of gods needed human sustenance? It was the dividing line between them and the God that I did believe in. I didn't dare suggest that the village pray and fast to hear from our God instead, but I could at least scoff at their existing traditions.

I thought about how the chief priest even heard these gods of his when he prepared to speak to the chiefs and his king or if he just decided that the gods had said whatever he liked and then came trotting in the sun and sand with it in his left hand.

All the good that God and Civilization would do to this place.

It was late evening when Aaliyah crawled into the room where I lay alone. She was the youngest of Baba Ibeji's wives and the only one who didn't wear the white wrappers and beads that the other wives of Obas did. The girl hardly ever spoke unless spoken to and kept to herself at all times. Her eyes always looked dull and far away, as though she had lent us her body, but her mind and soul had a different life on another plane.

Tonight, she was dressed in a patterned wrapper that she had knotted on her shoulder, and her feet were bare and dusty. Her small fingers toyed with the braids on her hair, loosening apart the tighter ones that pulled against her scalp. She bowed in greeting, and I nodded back, but no words passed between us till she sat on the floor.

"Tunde is going to become the king?" She asked in Yoruba. It was the first time she and I had ever conversed alone, and I was taken aback, unsure of if it was even allowed. Her voice sounded louder in the enclosure of the room, as though the mud clumps that made up the walls were her friends, and itched for her softened voice to pour into the tiny holes the night breathed through like a sleeping child.

I remained unsure if I was allowed to speak to her, so I cut my words short when I said, "Yes."

"Because of stranger with cutlass?" she attempted in English. I turned to her in confusion and repeated her words to her. She nodded without hesitation. She gestured with her hands as she tried to tell a story. "They come with cutlass and steal and fight in the night. They cover their head, and their mouth is black."

"Who is coming with cutlasses?" I asked. She started to speak, but her eyes glanced toward the door in a beat; someone had entered the room.

It was my brother; he stood resting against the patterned wrapper that served as a door and watched us. He turned to the girl and spoke in Yoruba. "The attackers that came that night."

She nodded and pointed to the makeshift door. "I show you where they burn when they come. Come and see."

She leapt to her feet like a cat and gestured for us to follow her. When she leapt into the night outside the hut, her small figure appeared lost in the darkness. Tunde followed after her, and I found that I did, too.

The night was dark, but my eyes adjusted quickly. The moon lit up the village, and smaller fires where people cooked and sat to talk cast shadows of them where I walked. I couldn't see Aaliyah in the dark and just followed my brother's footsteps. I remembered how his feet never seemed to follow each other in a straight gait, the result of a failed backflip off the water tank and onto his ankle as a child.

I had been a more simple child. Obedient and without the desire to leap off random objects till I shattered a bone with a name I couldn't spell. My mother believed that it was because she had prayed for a girl when she was pregnant with Tunde, so God had answered her with a willful boy. And having learned her lesson with me, she had simply asked that his will be done, and he had given her a softer son.

"Ibi ti won jona niyi. The place where they set fire" She pointed out a section of the village where the moonlight was undeterred by trees and huts. It was a mountain of ashes, and the silver seemed to glow in the moonlight. Aaliyah bends to scoop the ash in her hands gently and holds it to Tunde's face. The night wind doesn't allow him to look down on it for long before it blows it away to dance in the air.

"Was there anybody inside?" I asked in sickly-sounding Yoruba. She nodded, her voice choking up with emotion. "Small children, *meji*. Plenty goat. Some woman. They take some away and leave remaining to burn inside fire."

"Thank you," Tunde said to her and bent down to sift through the ashes. I follow suit and coat my hands in the soot 'til my hands are lost. The ashes are spread across the open land and toward the trees, like a scar on the land. Some belongings are still strewn in the ashes, but they are hard to make out in the darkness and the expanse of the dirt. I wonder which of them belonged to the babies that had died in the fire.

"I go back now. You, stay," Aaliyah replied and struggled to her feet. I saw for the first time that her shoulders appeared heavy as if she were carrying the weight of an invisible world.

I stood to my feet and apologized to Aaliyah with my eyes. She smiled softly, and briefly, I found it hard to swallow. My eyes travelled to the curve of her mouth and then the skin of her bare shoulders before I caught myself and stopped. She walked away, returning to where we came from, brushing me lightly as she did.

"Why person go come kill small children?" Tunde asked, and I couldn't recognize the emotion that now clogged his voice. Tunde never cried; he was always too busy laughing.

"I don't know," I replied. I never had an answer to questions about why people did things they did; it was difficult enough to find out why I did some of the things I did. "Let's go. I don't think we're supposed to stay here."

He nodded and dusted off the ash on his fingers, loudly clapping his hands against themselves. I left the blackness on my fingers, dusting it off, and felt like I was forgetting what I had just seen.

What did those children do to deserve this? Did they even know what was happening as the fire engulfed them?

We walked toward one of the open flames in a corner next to where other animals were kept, the smell of faeces and manure filling the air. The buzzing of insects would grow, imitating the hum of our refrigerator back home. I couldn't look into the fire for too long; the duller glow of orange seemed to morph into the shape of a sleeping child when I did.

Tunde sat on the sand by the fire, and I joined him. My brother's gaze was fixed on the flickering flames that surrounded the sacred circle of glowing embers of burning wood. The light danced in his eyes, casting an ethereal glow that masked the gravity of the night's events. I could feel the weight of the impending burden of Tunde's new duties hanging heavily in the air like a storm cloud threatening to unleash its fury. What was he supposed to do about the bandits that had come to wreak havoc on the village? Fight them?

I cleared my throat, my voice betraying a mix of apprehension and nostalgia. I did not know how to begin, but the words spun themselves like a baby spider's web. "Do you remember that cybercafe that used to be in front of the house? In Oke-Ira?"

Tunde's lips curled into a faint smile, a flicker of the mischievous boy from our childhood. "Ah, Onome's cyber cafe. How I go forget?"

I nodded, a bittersweet pang tugging at my heart. Onome was a short teenager who was tasked with running his mother's cybercafe when Tunde and I were children. He walked with his shoulders raised like there was a boil under his armpits that kept him from bringing them down.

"When you started duplicating the internet pin for the computers without paying."

Tunde chuckled softly. "When Onome found out, he come dey shout dey chase us with those his short legs."

"Then I fell into the gutter, that big one with green water," I said, a playful grin tugging at the corners of my lips. I recalled coming home, dripping from head to toe in algae and torn nylon bags. Daddy had asked me to stand outside the house and use the water hose for the car to rinse the muck off me before I even thought of touching the handle of his house door. It was one of the days I swore off accompanying Tunde on any of his adventures again.

Tunde's expression turned contemplative, his gaze distant for a moment. "This Oba thing still never clear for my eyes, because I no even expect am. Now I don see wetin cause am, and my hands just dey shake."

I felt a lump form in my throat, understanding the weight of his words. "Be like say you sef don get big things for your hands now."

The pidgin was raw in my throat. Although she wasn't present, I could hear my mother berating me for wasting the school fees she paid just to come out and speak like a novice. She had given up on getting Tunde to only speak English; he spent too much time with his friends who only spoke pidgin, and it often came out even when he didn't mean it to.

Tunde's eyes met mine, a mixture of emotions swimming within them. Probably the most I had ever seen in his yellowed eyes. "Omo, but I go just dey this village. Far from everything, I go just dey wear crown dey shake one horsetail. I never even know wetin I suppose do for this bandits wey come steal and burn. Na me go fight them?"

I placed my hand on his shoulder and noticed for the first time that it shook, but I kept it in place. I hoped he could see it as a gesture of comfort and my solidarity. "You don become big man now, Layo sef go dey reason herself if she hears am."

He offered a half-smile, and his eyes glowed in the light of the flame as his mouth morphed to allow a short laugh. "Shey, you go call am tell her, Leye? You fit just call am say, You know say Tunde don be Oba for our town now."

"For sure."

As the night fire burned lower, a part of me wondered if perhaps in months and years to come, and on days when Tunde and I were hundreds of kilometres apart and thought of each other, the shared memories would be what connected us. If somehow, I thought of a memory and he remembered it at the same time, I would get goosebumps or some other confirmation that he was thinking of me as well.

That night would pass, and then an afternoon would be spent preparing for a coronation ritual before my faith in those memories would be shaken. The night of the coronation ritual was a new night with a seemingly new darkness; this darkness was nothing like the darkness of the night before, which would be spotted with lights from time to time. It was near complete darkness, the kind that formed its faces and shapes for those who had things to run from.

Tonight, girls were not allowed outside, and neither were their mothers, not on nights like these.

The night breeze carried the scent of blood and doom. I could not be sure if it was the wind that made me feel as cold as I did or the fear that had its hands around my face. All of its bony fingers were stuffed down my throat, keeping me from speaking or breathing too loudly. I was simply present.

Tonight, what was left of the lights that kept our rural kingdom lit now cast our shadows. All of our shadows stretched from our feet to where Tunde lay bare on the ground in the centre of our circle. Chiefs, Priests, fathers, and sons were all dressed in white garbs, and all our shadows bore the same contorted black outline.

Tunde lay unmoving on the ground as we waited for the final part of the rites. Ifagbemi leaned over my brother and brandished a short knife from his robe. Quickly and firmly, he sliced a killing cut along Tunde's throat and clamped a hand over his mouth to keep him from screaming. A cold shiver ran down my spine, and I fought the impulse to leap to stop the bleeding. I have been warned countless times before of the steps of this ritual. It does not make it much easier, however.

In the dim light of the flames, the sacrifices that the gods deemed vital to the birthing of any new king shone brightly. Our oblations were the yellow of the *egusi* that Oyedele had stewed for the gods and my bleeding brother. The lacerated cut across Tunde's throat had bled out onto the sand quickly.

I knew I was supposed to keep my eyes closed while we waited, but I lacked the discipline. I needed to see the moment when my brother would rise with his wounds healed. I was forced to trust Ifagbemi, the archaic priest; they claimed he had never been a man who lied or failed despite his primitive belief in wooden gods.

Minutes passed, and my brother was yet to budge, so my gaze found my grandfather, Baba Ibeji. I looked over his loosely hanging clothes to his left hand where three fingers hung limp; the other two now apparently belonged to the bandits. I often wondered what the bandits did with the fingers they tore off the former Oba; Perhaps one of them hung it around his neck for show. Guns and cutlasses could no longer protect the people of our village, and neither could Baba Ibeji. It was for this purpose that they needed a new king.

The kind of king whose magic would make our men vanish before their attackers. The kind of godlike king whose magic swept into our crippled market to draw traders to our village. Tunde would be the vessel for such a king.

In the sand where Tunde lay bound by physical ropes and abstract binds of duty, like Japanese Shibari, he reminded me for the first time of his son, when the little boy was wrapped and swaddled in clothes after his birth.

We stood and waited for the last part of our coronation rituals to bear fruit, for the moment when our king whose throat we had slit would rise from his baptism of blood with the tongues of our forefathers on his lips. We waited till the sun broke and the morning breeze blew out our torches, but our king never arose.

Rather than bring back the ancestors, Tunde had gone on to join them.

In the hours that followed, only grief and panic

followed for the ones that we had lost and the ones that we would lose again when we failed to defend the village from the attackers.

UNHOLY MATRIMONY

- Praise Abraham

Lucy felt the path of the slimy liquid as it worked its way down from her head to her throat.

Somehow, instead of just washing over her body, it penetrated through the layers of her skin.

When it reached her taste buds, she could swear it tasted of the rottenest food she had ever seen or smelt. The problem was, as much as she wanted to gag, she couldn't. The slime was filling her up, leaving no room for an outlet.

She was locked in a room. A dark, musky room where dim rays of yellow, fluorescent light pierced through slanted cracks on the raftered window. The light provided no relief. It only helped to increase the eeriness of the shadows that danced on the walls and ceiling of the room.

A distant echo of slowly dripping water became pronounced.

Drip! Drip! Drip!

The sound changed as it drew closer.

Tap! Tap! Tap!

It was the sound of bare feet padding on a wet surface.

"Missed me?" a saccharined voice purred from the shadows.

'No, no, no! Not again!'

Lucy shook her head vigorously and began to squirm and wiggle to break free, only to realise her body was wrapped in an invisible barrier.

Panic spread from her chest to her entire system.

The malevolent being in the shadows tsked.

She could sense him circling her like a prowling lion that was assessing the target prey it was about to pounce on. The motion gave her mega-sized goosebumps on her arms.

"Are you trying to hide from me, pumpkin?"

His masculine form sauntered towards her heaving form, twirling a sharp, glistening knife in his hand. He stepped into the tiny ray of light, looking almost perfect, like a magazine-worthy badass model. If not for the wicked slits in his irises that were pronounced by the mischievous grin on his flawless lips, he would have been perfect.

Lucy had sworn, a long time ago, when this harmless imaginary friend had begun to show his true dark colours, that she would not be deceived by whatever false mask he came with.

She was now well acquainted with what lay beneath the attractive facade.

Even though she knew what would come next, nothing could prepare her for the new degree of torment he came up with each time he showed up, which had been more frequent lately.

She gulped in gasps of air and fought harder.

"Oh! Aren't you a scared*y* kitten? You know you are mine, don't you? Why try to fight me? Simply yield, and I promise this will be a smooth ride."

He leaned forward and grinned into her alarmed face. His chilly breath assaulted her nostrils.

He placed the tip of the knife on her cheek. Lucy sucked in her breath and closed her eyes. A lone tear escaped.

"Dioni, please, don't... Please just let me go!" she squeaked in terror.

She could sense his signature smirk even with her eyes closed. He was probably thrilled that she had uttered his name.

Lucy remembered how he told her his name. It had been under the most romantic circumstances.

She was about twelve at that time. Yes, twelve and all alone in the world. It was her birthday.

He had given her a rose. The thorns pierced her skin and drew blood as an accompaniment to the gift of her knowing his name. It had been a lovely dream. The loveliest she'd had since her entire family died in a car crash.

"My precious pumpkin. You are going nowhere. And you are well aware of that."

While her eyes were still closed, she began to hear the signature crackle-pop-snap sounds of Dioni's shape-shifting. Some seconds later, the sound stopped.

"Look at me." His voice came out in a low growl.

She shut her eyes tighter, her heart pounding like a jackhammer. There was no prayer on her lips. It was pointless. Besides, why would a God above care about a hag below like her? She was too filthy and was deserving of this torment.

KEPRESSNG

"I said, 'look at me'!" Dioni's growl was more guttural and fierce now.

Startled by the pressure of the knife that had now slid to her throat and the trickle of warm blood that had already begun worming its way down to her chest, she gasped, and her eyes opened.

Lucy immediately regretted her choice. She wished she could become blind forever if only to escape the terrifying sight before her eyes.

In place of his comely features, there was a mask of leathery skin marred with different scars and tattoos; golden eyes, glinting like a cat's, bore into her wide-as-saucer eyes; a slithering forked tongue flickered, licking her cheek as though tasting her; his breath smelt sulphurous and stale, like the slime that she was currently doused in.

As the pressure of the knife on her neck intensified, Lucy let out an ear-splitting scream from the depths of her being.

It was impulsive and pointless. No one would hear.

This was her never-ending cycle. She was trapped here in God-knew-where with this demon that had oscillating mood swings.

Still, she screamed her lungs out.

Faintly, as though from a thousand light years away, she felt the tapping of fingers on her right shoulder.

"Lucy? Lucy! Wake up!"

Her eyes flew open.

With loud gasps and breaths, she struggled to get a hold of what was reality—the fading scene of death versus the familiar view of her most recent workplace.

KEPRESSNG

Oh, she was still at work. The blue rays of her desktop computer illuminated her face.

It was Joshua who had woken her up, saving her from further disgrace.

Her eyes darted around like a pendulum bob. Only a few workers glanced at her curiously. Others remained focused on their business.

Joshua looked a bit spooked by her state.

"Are you okay? You've been mumbling in your sleep."

She couldn't respond.

No, she was not okay. Something strange was happening.

Not the fact that a familiar and very dangerous demon from her past had resurfaced - that was normal, somewhat.

It was the fact that he had come during the day.

He normally came at a specified time—around three in the morning—when she was asleep. The borders between her dreamscape and reality would merge, and she would either wrestle or submit to this demon till daybreak.

Daytime was the only time she would then sneak an hour or two to sleep, during any break time she could get.

Every night, she would set her alarm to 2 am to avoid the dream encounters with Dioni. Sometimes it worked. Sometimes, nature said, 'no!'.

Lucy felt her eyes would pop out any minute.

She didn't have a wink of sleep last night.

This morning at the cyber cafe where she had just been newly employed, her grumpy boss handed her a pile of manuscripts to transcribe with a deadline that was fast approaching.

KEPRESSNG

She couldn't dare to say no.

Finding and keeping a steady job had been one of her major challenges. She wouldn't allow anything, not even her current secret torment, to take her only source of livelihood from her.

"Lucy! Are you really okay?" Joshua asked again, concerned.

"I said I'm fine!" she snapped at him.

"Okay. Sorry," he replied in a hurt tone.

Lucy felt a pang of guilt.

After an awkward silence, she sighed and muttered, "I'm sorry, okay. It's just that..."

"No, no. No worries. I understand," he said quickly.

As Lucy stared into his warm brown eyes, she felt a strange peace wash over her. It was brief, but it had been such a long time since she felt anything this close to serenity that she was startled. Not since her world turned upside down after everything turned its back on a little orphan girl like her.

What did Joshua carry to have this effect on her? She'd known him for barely a week. Maybe she could trust and tell him about her hidden struggle.

Pronged doubts rose to squelch that idea. In her teen years, she had been foolish to open up to her paternal uncle about the imaginary friend who always came to visit her. Then, Dioni began to get violent.

That stupid uncle had only taken advantage of her fear and vulnerability and had molested her, opening the gate for more demons to accompany Dioni to strengthen his hold on her.

No way would she permit a repeat of that.

"Are you done with your assigned work?" Joshua asked as he rose from his seat beside hers.

"No," she replied in a weary drawl. "Still have a

long way to go."

Joshua gave her a sympathetic look.

She stretched on the chair. She'd been asleep for...

What? Five minutes? Her permanent eye bags must be so much more aggravated now, she was sure. It was high time she took a break.

When she stood up, she noticed that her feet had swollen slightly. Tiny electric surges flowed through her feet, momentarily stopping her movement short.

She muttered a cuss word and proceeded to move to the kiosk outside to see if she could get a snack or something to eat.

She hadn't had a proper meal today, and it was almost closing hours already.

There was no way she would proceed with her work - about twenty-five more pages to type a dissertation for a client –without imploding with hunger.

Outside, the muted colours of sunset had begun their splash motion over the canvas of the sky.

"Nice view, uhm?" Joshua's voice crooned close to her ear.

Startled, she jumped. She hadn't known that he was following her.

"Sorry. Didn't mean to scare you."

She gulped and nodded; his proximity brought eerie memories.

"Want to get something?" he asked, gesturing towards the crowded kiosk ahead.

She nodded.

They began to stroll in sync to the booth where they could grab a snack.

Joshua was silent all through. She knew he was very worried but he didn't say anything more.

Ever since she came here, he had been indirectly watching out for her. Whispered rumours around the Cafe made her aware that he was the 'preacher boy' in this workplace who had been kicked out of his former job at a bar for proselytising.

She strongly suspected that his interest in her was the trigger for the re-emerging of Dioni.

Dioni hated it whenever she got slightly close to any human of the male species, not to talk of one who was a Christian. She tried not to think about the terror that awaited her at home tonight.

In the end, she couldn't eat the snack Joshua eventually insisted on buying for her. Her stomach was tied in a twisted knot of worry, and her appetite had vanished.

She lingered at her workplace, knowing that evil awaited at home. Instead of packing up fast and going home at the same time as the other workers, she asked permission from her boss to work overtime. The man was happy to oblige.

Before Joshua left, he paused, gave her a prolonged gaze and said, "Lucy, I don't have any idea what you're going through. Even if anyone does, the person might have no definite solution to offer you. But there is One who does. And He cares for you."

She didn't respond to his preaching. Even though he respected everyone's personal space and didn't try to shove his religion down anyone's throat, his life bore enough proof of what he believed if one counted his overworn clothes and scrawny figure as proof.

But Lucy knew Dioni was too powerful. She was his sacrificial lamb. According to the mantra he indoctrinated her with, she'd been married off to him by her paternal great-grandmother, and nothing in heaven or earth could break that bond.

At 9 pm she knew she had to leave the cafe because the area hooligans had begun their nightly business. The vicinity was not safe for a lady to be alone. She switched off the system she'd been robotically typing on for hours on end, turned off the single bulb that was on, and securely shut down the garage door of the Cafe.

She shuffled to her house just two streets away, passing the dark, lonely path that was the only road to her destination. The night was moonless. A good or bad sign? She wasn't sure.

A crunching sound a little distance behind her caused her to halt and turn, her heart pounding and her palms sweaty.

There was nothing, no monster stalking her. Only shadows.

Get a grip, Lucy.

Heaving a sigh of relief, she resumed her journey, this time walking faster.

The boys' quarter, where she'd been staying for the past year, was always too quiet, thanks to her never-present landlord, who didn't care to gather more tenants that he couldn't monitor.

Lucy's hands shook as she fished her keys from her bag to unlock the door. She knew round two of her doomsday was just about to begin.

Of course, thanks to the power distribution company's usual bad habit, the tiny space she called home was pitch black.

Since she didn't have a phone she could use as a temporary flashlight, she was forced to grope about the almost empty space in search of her battery-powered torch, hoping she'd left it on the table beside the door.

Just as she placed her hand on the table to get the torch, from nowhere, a cold, scaly hand grabbed and squeezed her hand.

Her heart lurched to her throat, and her breathing stopped. Her eyes almost swallowed her entire face with how wide they immediately went. She'd recognise that touch anywhere. Ninety-nine per cent of the time, it was restricted to the confines of her nightmare.

But seriously, weirder things were happening. Dioni had come to torment her by day. He was here physically, crossing the borders before the allotted time. Only once had that happened before, and that was when she returned a smile to a boy who had sent her a love letter in her junior year.

The next day, after a whole night of unexplainable physical battling, she came down with a terrible fever. It was one of the biggest lessons she'd learnt—Never provoke Dioni by hinting the slightest interest in the opposite sex.

Right now, she stood frozen in the darkness.

His face came only inches away from hers, this time without the fine mask.

Hideous. Grotesque. Shriek-worthy!

But Lucy knew screaming her lungs out, if she could, was pointless. No one would hear.

"Let's play a little game, sweet pumpkin." He smirked in satisfaction at her revulsion.

"It's called catcha-catcha!"

He flung his knife up in a dexterous throw and caught it again by the hilt several times.

"And guess who gets the honour of being the ball?"

Lucy began crying. Wracking sobs shook her body.

'Can anybody hear me? Please save me! I can't continue like this,' she cried out in her mind because her mouth was frozen.

"Oh, Lu! No one can save you. How many times do I have to iterate it? Until you accept that fact and choose to willingly obey me, I'll have no other option but to teach you the hard way."

And then, it began. The throwing. It was as though he grew ten times larger and she, as small as a racquetball in his hand.

He physically threw her all over the room until she felt blood cover her everywhere. Her muscles were so sore she couldn't feel them anymore. All her bones felt like they were mashed cheese balls being shaken in their pack.

Worn worse than the shoe of a desert traveller who had been on the road for months, she lay on the cold concrete floor, barely breathing.

The demon stood over her crumpled-on-the-floor body in triumph.

Suddenly, the door swung open. Shocked, she and Dioni looked towards the door. Someone was pointing a torch at her face, so she couldn't see who it was at first.

"Lucy? Oh my God, Lucy! What happened?"

That voice... Familiar. The person drew near in alarm and tried to help her sit up.

It was Joshua. Could this get any worse?

She grunted as he came close.

Dioni was still there, but he had moved a considerable distance from Joshua, and he was steaming mad. It was obvious to Lucy that Joshua couldn't see Dioni as his eyes were fixed on poor her alone.

"What's happening? I felt a strong impression in my spirit to follow you home, that something was off. There was noise in your house, so I was forced to check it. You're bleeding. Let me take you to the hospital!"

She couldn't speak yet, so she tried to communicate by shaking her head vehemently and through her crazed eyes that he should back off. She had to prove to Dioni that she didn't like Joshua in the least bit, or else it would be the end of them both. When he came too close to try to clean off the blood on her face, with her peripheral vision, she saw that Dioni was livid. He was screaming obscenities at her, but she couldn't hear him. All she heard was this prolonged ringing sound in her ears. She wondered why he wasn't attacking Joshua.

Suddenly, she felt a strangling force on her throat and knew instinctively what was happening; another shade of Dioni's mood swing that she hadn't witnessed till now was unveiling itself. He was taking control of her body, manipulating her. Using her as a medium because, for some reason, he was too terrified to come against Joshua alone.

She was a ragged cloak Dioni had slipped into this time. She could feel the presence of his entity that oozed evil churning deep within her. She felt tendrils of pain as her hand, controlled by Dioni's malevolent force, smacked Joshua's cheek.

Joshua's tender hands held back hers.

"You're hurting yourself, Lucy. I'm here to help you."

Inside, her heart wept. Why didn't he just leave already? Why was he persistent? She could see the reddening of her finger marks on his cheek, but still, he ignored his pain and was instead concerned about her.

"Go! Now! Leave this place. She is mine," Dioni

spoke through her mouth.

A new light of understanding dawned on Joshua and sparkled through his eyes.

"Who are you?" he asked.

Dioni laughed as he staggered to his feet, pulling her battered body upright. His cackle was a metallic, drunken sound. Lucy squirmed inside.

"I command you to speak by the blood of Calvary!" Joshua said with authority.

Dioni screeched and slammed her body back to the floor. Hmm. That was new. Dioni never reacted like that to anything or anyone else.

"I am Dioni, her spirit husband. She was betrothed to me from birth! Leave if you don't want to see my wrath!" he growled through a frothing mouth.

"A higher power has come to set her free."

"No!"

Lucy felt it when Dioni switched his attention to her. He began to speak to her mind.

"Haven't I told you not to meddle with these kinds of nitwits? Haven't I? Now, you'll have to come to me. I have waited so long for the final consummation of our marriage. Your foolishness has hastened the day!"

Lucy was too weak to even protest.

"Lucy, I know you're there, and you can hear me. Don't listen to whatever lie he is feeding you with. You can be free. Your redemption has been paid for," Joshua murmured.

Dioni made her stagger back up. He reached for a knife on her table and began brandishing it threateningly.

"Lucy, please, don't." Then, pointing at her, Joshua said, "You demon, I command you out in the power and authority of the Lord of Host!"

KEPRESSNG

The knife clattered to the floor. As Dioni tore apart from her body with a disembodied shriek, Lucy felt as though her innermost being was being shredded to pieces.

She crumpled to the floor, weak and exhausted to her marrow. She could, however, still sense Dioni lurking in the shadows, waiting to pounce again. She was tired of the struggle.

Why not end it now and save yourself from the inevitable torment that would resume once Joshua left? she thought.

The knife was just within her reach. She stretched her hand and, without thinking, with the last iota of strength in her, she drove it in the direction of her abdomen. She heard the sound of metal piercing flesh, but the pain she expected was non-existent.

She opened her eyes, confused. Joshua was so close to her. There was a pained shock in his eyes.

She gazed down and saw that the knife, slightly grazing her abdomen, had cut deep into Joshua's hand. He'd used his hand as a shield over her belly.

She started crying. Tears fell from his eyes too.

"Lucy," he said in a fast-weakening voice. He was losing blood from the wound in his hand like a tap. "No greater love hath any man than this, that a man should lay down his life for his friend."

Joshua fell unconscious a few seconds later, leaning on her shoulder.

Lucy wept, her eyes out against his neck. She was weak. He was unconscious. They were both dying.

As she raised her head back up, that evil glint she was familiar with bore into her eyes. The sinister glow hovering above made a shiver run down her spine.

Dioni smirked, compounding her guilt and making her feel it was her fault.

She realised then that he had put those suicidal thoughts in her head.

"I'll be back, pumpkin!" Dioni telepathically said to her and vanished.

Her pain, both physically and emotionally, was so excruciating that she allowed the fluctuating darkness to engulf her.

PRAISE ABRAHAM, also recognized by her pen name PeculiarPraise, is a rapidly emerging Christian author. Beyond her prowess in novel writing, she showcases her versatility through short stories, scripts, blog posts, reviews, articles, poems, and more.

With a string of accolades to her name, Praise has garnered recognition for her captivating storytelling. Her award-winning narratives are readily available on prominent online platforms such as Amazon, Wattpad, Selar, Pabpub, and various other outlets.

When she's not immersed in the writing world, Praise reads, hones her design, or enjoying quiet moments in the 'Secret Place'.

A BUNCH OF JARGONS

- Chika Eunice Emmanuel

PRESENT DAY
I stood in front of my supervisor's office, quite nervous to enter. The air felt stifling, and I took in deep breaths in quick succession so that my lungs didn't feel too tight or constricted. I wrangled my hands and paced around the halls, mustering the courage to knock so as to alert him of my presence. He asked me to come by eight a.m. to submit the first three pages of my dissertation so he could either approve or reject it for preliminary defence. I took in a deep breath and rapped two short knocks on the mahogany door.

"Come in." He called out in a deep, sonorous voice.

"Here goes nothing," I said under my breath as I opened the office door.

"You can have your seat, Miss Osinaforbueze. I believe you are here to submit your dissertation on the impact of African traditions on Africans."

"Yes, sir," I replied, bringing out my work from my

tote bag while fumbling a little. I mistakenly hit the container of pens on his table, and I watched helplessly as they clattered on the floor.

"So sorry, sir. Don't know what has gotten into me today," I apologised as I picked up the pens from the container and set them back on the table. I rose to my full height and handed him the dissertation copy I held. I rubbed my clammy hands on my sky- blue coloured jeans as he began flipping the pages. My mind conjured different scenarios as he flipped through because I feared I was not submitting what my supervisor wanted to see. Some of the scenarios had him giving me a disappointed stare. I shuddered at the thought.

"You believe you captured all the beautiful things African tradition is, don't you?" he asked, setting the dissertation copy back on the table. I stared at it, and for a moment, it looked like it was taunting me.

"Well, I captured what resonated with me most," I stated - trying my best not to give so much away.

"I believe this will be a lovely read. Can't wait to delve in." He picked up my dissertation again.

"I hope so too. So, when can I come back for your feedback on the work, sir?" I asked.

"In two weeks' time, say Tuesday?" He replied.

"Okay, two weeks it is then." I stood up and walked out of the office.

DISSERTATION ENTRY
DECEMBER, 2021
When a woman is birthed, she is placed on a wall by society and pinned with the tip of an iceberg.

A woman's life is spent teetering and wobbling at

the blade's edge while society wields the sword.

She is reminded not to laugh too loudly so as not to appear uncouth.

She is warned not to be overly emotional, as no guy wants to marry an emotional baggage.

She is cautioned not to be too ambitious, as it is unbecoming. No one wants to marry a boss but a wife, she is told.

She is counselled not to speak in a gathering of men, as it's disrespectful.

She is urged not to argue with her husband, as it is rude. No one wants to marry a know-it-all.

From the moment she is birthed, she is displayed like market wares in hope that a buyer will find her worthy to be paid for and taken home to be used at his discretion.

She is trained to be prim and proper for a man who will grade her okay enough to be his wife.

She is not interested in cooking? Oh, the horror! Her husband and children will starve to death.

She is not keen towards hand washing? What a disgrace! What good wife makes use of a machine to do her family's laundry?

She is a bit of a scatterbrain and not good at house arrangement. No way! She must be good; else she will be chased back by her husband to her parents' house in disgrace.

A few women have unpinned themselves from this wall and have chosen to wield their own sword without validation from anybody.

These women have been seen as *A disgrace, Uncultured, Will never get married* by society.

I am one of those few women who has chosen to wield her own sword despite the tongue-lashing by society.

My mother named me, *Amuruijeozi,* meaning, *born to serve,* in our Igbo dialect.

She told anyone who cared to listen that I had always been unruly right from the womb. I kicked as hard as a boy, and since a scan for the reveal of a child's gender wasn't in vogue those days, there was no way of confirming my gender.

She and my father threw a party, thinking I was going to be a boy. Oh, the irony! Only to be disappointed after my birth to see I was a girl. After I was birthed, my mother failed to conceive again. She said my *chi* was too strong, and my personality was unable to take on another sibling.

On a bad day, she blamed me for her inability to conceive again.

She named me *Amuruijeozi* because she hoped it would tame down what she liked to refer to as my *brazenness.*

When I became older, I decided to change my name to *Osinaforbueze,* meaning, born *to lead.*

It made me feel strong, like I could conquer the world. So, allow me to reintroduce myself. My name is *Osinaforbueze,* and here are stories about key aspects of my life that shaped me into who I am today.

HARMATTAN SEASON
NOVEMBER – JANUARY 2002

The wind blew strongly, raising a lot of dust, and some people's skin became cracked and white, so one may fear skin disease. Yes, this was the harsh and popular season of harmattan in Nigeria. A season where parents lathered their children's skin with the local mix of *Ori* and *Vaseline* until their skin glistened like they hugged and shared a passionate kiss with the sun, while others looked like they ingested the famous sixty-watt yellow bulb.

It was during this period that I visited my aunt in Enugu from Lagos. I was so excited to see my aunt because Aunty Ada was a force to be reckoned with. She was one of those people who made you hold your breath as the wheels turned in your head, and your mouth became limp because of the inability to conjure up words that truly and accurately describe her.

I first met Aunty Ada when I was eight years old. My dad, though not one with a history of violence, hit my mom for the first time, and her left eye got swollen. My mom tried to downplay it when she told Aunty Ada, but Aunty Ada was not having it, so she took the next flight to Lagos.

When she arrived at the house, her eyes were blazing in anger that if they were actual guns, she would have shot my dad a couple of bullets. Her nose flared, and her lips thinned in disapproval as she yelled at my dad. At that point, I was honestly scared our roof was going to cave in due to the level of decibels her voice was raised to.

But I saw something spectacular that day. I saw my dad, a very confident man, cower at Aunty Ada.

I was captivated by the energy she emitted, and if someone asked little me what I wanted to be in life at that very moment, I would have replied, 'I want to be like Aunty Ada.'

Aunty Ada was the first to ever ask me, 'What do you think?'

I was so shocked by her question that I sputtered through my answer. I was so used to people telling me what to do and no one caring for my opinion.

KEPRESSNG

Aunty Ada just shook her head that day and said, 'You have a brain and a mouth. Use both.'

A lot of women found it demeaning to be referred to as a feminist, but not Aunty Ada.

She embraced being called a feminist with the famous *Naija* slang, *her full chest.*

Aunty Ada said her reason for being a feminist was when the world was formed, patriarchy took over, and the scale towards both genders was tipped in the disfavour of women.

If one unlucky person dared argue with her, she launched into her classic instance.

When a young, unmarried pregnant woman ventures out of her house, society spits at her and calls her loose. Everyone forgets that it also takes one morally loose guy to get her pregnant.

At this point, Aunty Ada says, 'After all, the girl is no Mary.'

Only the girl gets to carry the shame of what transpired in secret to the public's judging eyes.

Then she concludes, 'That, my dear, is why I am a feminist.'

I have never seen anyone argue with her after this classic example of why she's a feminist.

She loved people who read, so she got me Chimamanda Adichie's *Dear Ijeawele* for one of my birthdays.

I think the tousled pages and the cracked spine told how much I valued the book.

One glance at my birthday present, my mom groaned and said, 'You're instigating this girl's brazenness.'

'As it should be.' Aunty Ada replied, effectively shutting my mom up.

KEPRESSNG

Aunty Ada welcomed me heartily when I arrived at her house in Enugu.

For the past two weeks, we had the most fun. I learnt how to play Draft, Ludo, and even Whots.

Every night, we strolled and had the best *suya* around. Some nights, if we were feeling adventurous, we changed to another *suya* joint but quickly reverted to our usual one the next day.

Aunty Ada jokingly said, 'This *Aboki* don use juju hold us tight.'

All was going well in Eden until the devil decided he wanted to play.

One cold and lifeless Saturday morning, we woke up without any ill feelings lurking around. We didn't know that Death had clung its claws into our household. Aunty Ada and I had Akara and Pap for breakfast. We laughed heartily about anything and everything. From her neighbour who constantly spoke with a faux accent and constantly overpronounced the 'th' since returning from a two-week trip to London. Or the man who has refused to call Aunty Ada anything but 'Dear' ever since he found out Aunty Ada was unmarried despite him being married 'happily' with *tiri* beautiful children. He constantly mispronounced three and it was a thing of mockery between Aunty Ada and me.

When I got to the kitchen after breakfast, in a bid to heat up some water for bathing, I discovered our cooking gas was exhausted. I groaned and decided to ask Aunty Ada what we were going to do about it.

As I approached her room, I heard her phone ring.

It wasn't long before I heard a loud, piercing scream from her room. I knew from that moment sorrow had entered our house and clung to us like an unwelcome visitor who refused to leave.

When I got into the room, Aunty Ada could only mumble, 'Mama is dead'.

Death? Oh, what an unfriendly foe. It has come knocking thrice on our door. First, was Aunty Ada's husband, who died serving in the army. Second, was my mother, who died after losing her battle with cancer. Third was my grandmother, who died from the wiles of old age.

From that day, Aunty Ada's phone began ringing off the hook.

I was perplexed by the selfishness people exhibited. Questions such as, 'When will the burial be?' made me want to reply with 'She just died. Stop asking insensitive questions.' 'Have you started buying the *Aso-ebi*?' made me want to say, 'It's a burial, not a wedding ceremony'. Since when did a burial become about the colour scheme of *gele* or shoes you had at home?

Aunty Ada was pestered incessantly until she reluctantly fixed a date.

From this point, it was like Aunty Ada lost her identity; she was no longer opinionated about things, even when something as controversial as her neighbour's child getting pregnant out of wedlock and being called *loose* and *cheap* by the guy's mother happened in the environs while she was receiving the evening breeze I persuaded her to go out for. The woman's raised voice as she called the girl lots of demeaning names were lost to Aunty Ada's soulless stare into space. Even the girl's piercing scream was lost to Aunty Ada's deafened ears. I watched helplessly as society turned against the girl and made the guy a glorified martyr who was seduced by the girl's siren voice and mermaid curves.

The Aunty Ada I knew before would have flared up and said it takes two to *tango*. However, the Aunty Ada I saw now was muted by grief; tears were her nightly companion.

Seeing her running around to gather funds for the burial really broke my heart. I began to detest a tradition such as ours that put the living in so much debt in order to bury the dead.

I heard elders make statements like, 'Mama has to be sent properly.'

Sent where exactly? Since when did the dead care about how they are buried?

During the preparations for the burial, Aunty Ada's eyes cast shadows of grief, and her ever-smiling face developed worry lines.

During the burial week, I saw Aunty Ada in a dishevelled state as she was everywhere trying to piece everything together since she was the only surviving child from her parents, so she bore the whole burden.

I was so scared that Aunty Ada was slowly losing her identity.

The camel's back broke when Aunty Ada approached the council of elders concerning the burial arrangements. The oldest of the group said, 'Do not speak here unless you have a man that will speak for you.'

Aunty Ada's face steeled back to the woman I was once familiar with. I think she was sick and tired of being pushed around. 'I am the one burying my mother, and if I am not human enough to speak to you people, then to hell with you and your archaic traditions.'

They had no choice but to speak to Aunty Ada after

this.

I would never say that the burial went seamlessly; there were talks about her buying a very fat cow for the *Umuada*. Is the cow more important when someone has died? I mused to myself.

The evening after the burial, Aunty Ada finally settled down on the sofa.

I just went there and hugged her tightly because sometimes you do not need words to comfort someone. It was then Aunty Ada cried, really cried, for the death of her mother – for such a loss so great that she hasn't been able to grieve for.

As I held Aunty Ada limply in my arms, I realised something.

I didn't like this aspect of my culture. Where the living is taxed so much to bury the dead, and they are seen scurrying around to gather funds, that the death of their loved one never hits till after the burial.

I vowed never to let a tradition make me feel helpless.

RAINY SEASON
APRIL 29TH, 1996

I was an only child, but I grew up with two cousins. They lost both parents in a car crash, so it was agreed during the family meeting that my dad would take care of them. My cousins were fraternal twins, with a six-month gap between us. I remember always being in the kitchen helping my mom while they always went out to play with their friends. My mom never cautioned them to do otherwise.

I felt displeased at such action. Also, weren't they humans like me? Why do I have to be subjected to domestic chores, and they can just run around like a loose kite?

I decided to voice out my concerns one day. As a little girl of ten years, I too, wanted to play with my friends and hop around like a grasshopper with no restraint.

'Mum, why don't Peter and Paul assist us in the kitchen?' I questioned that hot afternoon as I sliced onions with tears streaming down my cheeks. Effect of the onions.

'Well, it's because you are a girl,' my mom answered like it was obvious.

But, it still wasn't making any sense to me. What had helping in the kitchen got to do with being a girl or a boy?

'I still don't understand.'

'It's a woman's job to cook, clean, and take care of the home,' Mom sighed and went back to chopping her *ugwu* like we just finished talking about the weather.

I remember detesting my cousins for being born so lucky. I cursed the stars that made me a woman.

I thought critically about it. I was told to bend my waist properly to sweep. Told to behave properly so my husband would not chase me back to my parents' house when I eventually got married.

I don't remember similar lessons being issued to my cousins. They weren't told that they needed to learn to treat their wives well or to love and cherish their wives.

I realised what the problem was. Then, I decided that whenever I had my own children, they both would learn equally the importance of treating one's spouse well.

No one is exempted from domestic chores. What is good for the goose is good for the gander.

RAINY SEASON
JUNE - OCTOBER, 2007

I worked briefly at a tech company during this time. I finished my first degree in Literature at the age of twenty-one, and I decided to go back to school to study computer science for a second degree.

During my third year, I went for my I.T. at a giant tech company owned by a powerful woman named Veronica Adegoke.

Veronica built her tech company from scratch but never got accolades. Her husband was given the accolades because, to society, it was, 'How could a mere woman build a company?' Meanwhile, in actual reality, it was when her husband lost his job that he started working in her company, so basically, her company gave him something to do. Whenever they walked past workers, only her husband was acknowledged, and she was ignored as if she were invisible.

Veronica brought up most of the tech ideas that pushed the company to the top form it was. It broke my heart that all her creativity was downtrodden to her husband's *help*.

It made me remember what I read in Chimamanda's *Dear Ijeawele,* where a woman's achievement was reduced to her husband, who *allowed* her to shine.

I then vowed to never let society pale my achievements to a man who *allowed* me to shine.

RAINY SEASON
MAY 15TH, 2010.

During this period, I learnt important lessons. When a man cheats on his wife, he would be cuddled; the wife would be told things, like, 'It's a man's nature to cheat', 'he tried being faithful to you for ten years', 'Just forgive for the sake of your children'.

When a woman cheats on her husband, the reverse is the case. She is called degrading names like *ashewo kobo kobo*, *loose woman*. It made me realise the scale never tipped in her favour. This period made me wish that both men and women were given the same scale of treatment after cheating on their spouses.

RAINY SEASON
MAY 20TH, 2020

This story was a dark moment in my life. Something quite ironic was that for a story that changed my life forever, I never knew the name of the woman that played the lead role.

I first got in contact with the unnamed woman one hot afternoon. She ran past me like a rabbit who was being chased by a hunter. I didn't know what was chasing her or even who was chasing her, but she ran like her life depended on it.

However, what I could never forget was the fear that shone in her eyes.

I later got to know that she had run away from her husband's house. Her husband was constantly hitting her, and she ran away for fear of her life. That evening, her mother and her mother's association of friends sat her down to advise her. I lent my ears in the hope they would advise her properly, but instead, I just heard *a bunch of jargon*.

'Just take the beating like a woman,' one suggested.

'Maybe you are not submissive enough,' another one chirped in.

'What you are playing with is someone else's prayer,'

someone said.

'Just so you know, I have called your husband to pick you up. He's on his way,' her mother declared like she just did her daughter a massive favour. Not even taking notice of the despair on her daughter's face.

Few moments later, a car pulled up, and I saw the reason for the fear in the woman's eyes come down from the car with an arrogant smirk plastered on his face and a wolfish glint in his eyes. He looked like a hunter that just got his prey. I saw the woman shrink too many sizes too small as he led her to the car while her eyes begged her mother to save her. Yet, her ignorant mother just bid her bye. A few weeks after witnessing this scene, I heard the woman committed suicide.

I remembered how her eyes expressed fear, sorrow and anguish. I wondered if those eyes ever crinkled in excitement. Her mother wailed the loudest at her burial. I was appalled by such hypocrisy. I pitied her son, who stared into space with such empty eyes. He may never understand why the world was so unfair to his mother.

After some months, I heard the man remarried. Then, I began to pity the woman who had been saddled with such unfortunate fate unknowingly.

After that, I wished she wouldn't end up like the first.

DRY SEASON
FEBRUARY, 2022

I am currently studying African Culture and Practices for my PhD. For my thesis, I have chosen to put together these barbaric customs and traditions and title them, *A Bunch of Jargon*.

My project supervisor might have a heart attack or

two that my dissertation doesn't glorify my culture but instead criticises it.

However, it's time we tore up the old rulebook handed to us from previous generations and write ourselves a new one.

Those old rules are, after all, nothing but *a bunch of jargon.*

CHIKA EUNICE EMMANUEL, affectionately known as Emma Eunice, is a writer dedicated to infusing African Fiction with her unique flair and a burning passion to celebrate her originality.

Currently pursuing a law degree, Chika can often be found immersed in legal texts and sections of the Constitution. However, when she takes a break from her legal studies, she finds solace in the pages of romantic comedy novels or loses herself in the act of pouring her heart onto paper through her writing.

TO KILL A SINGLE YORUBA WOMAN

- Oluwabunmi Adaramola

5:30 am
You wake up every day at five-thirty AM, the loud emptiness beside you starkly reminiscent of your singleness. Of course, this is not the only thought on your mind, but recollections of your mother's regular and incessant cry every day she calls, that *her enemies want to succeed* in causing your marital delay, always supersede the more important voices in your head.

Your alarm rings loudly beside you, and you smile. Remembering the day two years ago when you decided on a whim to swap your phone alarm for a physical alarm clock in hopes that it would induce more discipline in your phone habits. It had been your goal, starting the new year, to develop a more consistent routine as opposed to the muddiness that defined most of your adulthood. Every day when you wake, you kneel beside your bed and say a quick morning prayer–wading through the feelings of pretence and predictability–before continuing your three-part bed, bath, and skin routine. And before you can get up from your prayer stance, your phone rings.

Glancing at the ID, you know your day would not be without its hitches because the person calling has a deft way of ruining your mood. For a minute or two, you decide to let the phone ring, mentally calculating how much time needs to pass before you can fire off a flaccid *"didn't see your call"* message. Releasing a resigned sigh, you slide the answer bar, knowing that should you miss her call, the whole family–especially your cousins in Canada–will hear of how rude and thoughtless you are.

"Good morning, Aunty," You respond politely, tucking the phone in the crook between my ear and shoulder as you begin the mundane task of laying the bed. You ignore her forced pleasantries, knowing it's merely a script she follows whenever she calls–her weak attempt at easing you into the real reason for her early morning disturbance. You know this because she does so every time and has her tells. Whenever she asks, '*How are you?*' what she really means is, '*Are you seeing anyone?*'

So when she does that, you shift the topic to another she's also quite fond of: *money*. And you latch on to her statement about BJ asking for an iPhone for Christmas, which you agree to get for him, in hoping this would placate her and her disruptive line of questioning. You hear the giddiness in her tone as she profusely thanks you, and you can almost taste the greed in her words as she reminds you that the new harvest offering is due on the upper Sunday of the month. Yet again, you ignore her words as you trudge listlessly to the bathroom, her next words stopping your movement abruptly.

"But you know, my dear, money is not everything in life *o*! *O ti o*, because whether you like it or not, it's not your pillow that will make your body feel satisfied when you come back from work each night, neither is it money that will comfort you!"

You laugh internally, not wanting to insult her by reminding her that it is this same money she shames you for having that forced her into an over twenty-year loveless marriage with Chief Oyebọ́lájí. You're thankful she did not insist on a video call this time around because if she had, it would have been difficult for you to control the mirth that forms in your eyes.

You mute yourself and laugh not because her words are funny but because her words' irony and delusion amuse you. Aunty Wonu had married a wealthy, decorated man—more than twenty-five years older than her—at the age of twenty, not because she loved or even respected him, but simply because of her greed and personal desire to fall in line with the elite socialite Lagos women she'd envied growing up. Yet, no matter how much she climbed to the top, there was always something to complain about, *Chief.*

You had overheard conversations she had with your mother when you were ten. She complained about *Chief's* persistent habit of lathering her face with sloppy spit-filled kisses–a telltale sign that he wanted to *do*–and then grunting his release thirty seconds after he lay on her and snoring not up to a minute later, with no care for her satisfaction. How she could only ever find pleasure in the arms of Sunday–the weekend cleaner who took special care of the house and her body–and how the money *chief* doled on her only seemed like a prison. You release a pang of laughter before unmuting yourself because you do not want her to know that you know she had never once experienced sexual satisfaction in her marriage with Chief, nor did his money console her, in contrast to the words she now threw at you.

"But, Aunty," You finally say, your tone placating. "Isn't it better to use dollars to fan yourself or spray it beside you in bed for comfort instead of crying over one useless man like that?" You can tell she feels the sting from your words because of how her breathing grows heavier and punchier.

"Do you remember Deaconess Yetunde? The one that all her children are now abroad?"

She doesn't allow you to confirm whether you do before she continues, faux excitement colouring her tone as she brushes over your awkwardly true statement and the lingering embarrassment she'd felt afterwards.

"Her son just came back to Nigeria for the holidays. Very handsome and well-brought-up man, and he's even around your age *o. Bi ti* like thirty-seven… thereabout. And he's very single. I will send him your number now so he can call you."

You mute the phone once again and release a loud, frustrated groan because it would not be the first time she's tried to set you up with a *friend's* son. It was her modus operandi from the day you turned twenty-five three years ago. Aunty Wonu always knew the son of her former classmate or *Chief's* longtime friend, who was single and itching to settle down. Of course, she'd be quick to dismiss the fact that they were always over fifteen years older than you were and only sought a wife to wear as a trophy in public and subject to a glorified modern slave in private. They were the type of men who chortled nauseating belly laughs over bottles and glasses of beer, loudly proclaiming that a woman's value was in when she married and the type of man that deemed her worthy for marriage to them.

"Aunty—" You know she can hear the frustration in your tone, but she pretends, decidedly intending to force her agenda on you before she leaves you to continue your day.

"Don't argue with me Irémidé o! You know you'll soon be thirty; your biological clock is ticking fast *o*! By the time you reach thirty, you will born *o ma* hard *gan o*! At least pity the kneeling of your mother; pity the thousands of hard currency your father has poured on your head to give you that fancy education you wield as a weapon against men in this Lagos!" Her final stamp—the emotional blackmail. She was a pro at it, and because you knew she would never stop if you interrupted and countered her points, you let her go on, pretending that all was okay.

But you knew—she'd once again successfully ruined another morning for you and were convinced she was after your life.

8:00 am
You notice the Toyota car beside you and the driver's attempt to overtake you on the already tight lane as you inch closer to the Lekki-Ikoyi link bridge—the unwilling main character in many recent Nollywood movies. You've been driving in Lagos for over three years now, and by now, you're used to the modus operandi of Lagos drivers in the event you allow even

one car to overtake you. So you prove stubborn by driving dangerously close to the car in front of you so that Mr Toyota does not bully you—you're nearly late to work anyway, so you have the time to engage his *werey*.

Mr Toyota's glare becomes angrier the more it lingers on you, and the merciless way he pounds his horn for you to 'give way' so he can enter. He can horn till tomorrow for all he likes, but you know giving in and allowing him to assert his delusional dominance on the road will only feed his ego, empowering him to act high and mighty throughout the day. So you take one for the team and refuse to give in because this morning, you have the time of men like him.

From the corner of your eye, you watch the person in Mr Toyota's passenger seat roll his window down and reduce the loud croons of the on-air personality from what you recognise as Cool FM. You can tell that they're both much older men, seated comfortably in Uncle Ogidiran's generation—the sandals on the passenger princess' feet and how they glare at you in expectation of a greeting and recognition of their older status, give it away. So you look ahead, holding on to the steering wheel—and your pride—as you pointedly ignore any staring contest they intend to initiate.

"Young lady," the nearest voice to me—the uncle in the passenger seat—screams loudly, forcing his voice to be louder than the ongoing commotion in the traffic.

You bite back the ire you would usually throw because of home training before you finally turn to them.

"*Iwo ni m'on ba soro o*! Is you I'm speaking to!" he continues in an angry tone as he switches to heavily accented Yoruba, a behaviour typical of older Yoruba men, who assume that because their tongues have been locked in their mother tongue, then everyone else must understand their language, whether they liked it or not.

"Sir?" Your tone lifts to a respectful level as you school your expression to one of docility, knowing that it is the best way to placate his emotion.

Mr Toyota leans forward and points a finger at you, "I don dey talk say women no fit drive for this Lagos! After all, na your husband's car be dis, una go dey form like say you fit drive like man, *radarada oshi!*" He hisses loudly, nearly spitting in the mouth of the passenger princess before rolling the window and speeding off ahead of you in a bid to enter the lane ahead.

You roll your head and close your eyes as you swallow yet another insult from Lagos drivers in traffic— who were quick to assume that you had walked into your non-existent husband's room to leisurely pluck a car key from the cupboard filled with keys, quickly disregarding any thought that perhaps personal ambition and hard work got you this 2020 Mercedes Jeep. After all, you were a woman who either had to open her legs or latch on to another man to enjoy the pleasures of life. You could build wealth, invest in real estate, become the youngest richest woman in the country and earn seats at global tables, but so long as there was no man—more so an obvious man bankrolling you—your existence would only be deemed insignificant.

Rolling your window back up, you release yet another sigh in traffic and push ahead.

9:30 am

KEPRESSNG

Patrick Akinfewa was the randiest man among the partners at Steinhart & Grey LLP, and you had the unfortunate pleasure of working with him in the corporate department. As you push the glass door to his office, clutching the report close to your chest, you remember the way he consistently comments on your outfit whenever you see him, incessantly reminding you that 'your *bumbum'* had a rude habit of entering his eye. *Today is no different,* you realise, as you watch his eyes rove hungrily over your body, sloppily wetting his lips. And as you nod at him after he smiles toothily at you, beckoning you to enter all the way into his office while he takes much effort to lift his tightly tucked frame from his chair, you remember how livid you had been the other time when he'd dragged your hand and forced you onto his laps as you lowered the previous report to his desk.

This time around, his stomach leads the way as he inches around the desk, and he smiles toothily at you, eyes trained on the beige silk shirt covering your chest. "Don't be difficult, sweet Iré. And this one that you're squeezing face this early morning, you better smile before you chase men away *o.*"

"I hope you are doing well this morning, sir. I hope you're great," you respond politely and rhetorically, ignoring his endearment. You'd mastered the art of deflecting, forcing yourself to become more or less used to it – his position had compelled you to accept it as a norm from him.

"Sir, I have our team's monthly report in hard copy as you requested."

Mr Patrick's lack of acceptance of technology and the digital age the company was now in had become burdensome to the entire team, where you were forced to submit reports and draft agreements in hard copy, spending a ridiculous amount of money on printing alone. At this point, it was almost a certainty that in the entire firm, your department used the most percentage of the budget on printing and paper costs alone.

"So you will not smile for me, Iré?? Or come closer to greet me?"

"No, thank you, sir, I'm fine where I am. I'll just leave it with your receptionist."

He twirls leisurely on his five-wheeler chair and points in my direction, "You and this, my receptionist. It's like you like her more than me. Don't be difficult, now, Iré. And I missed you this weekend *o.*"

You maintain your rather stoic expression for fear that a more pleasant body language may be misconstrued in the way he wants it.

"I trust your weekend was great, Mr Patrick. If you don't have any other information for me, I'll take my leave now. Alternatively, we can continue this discussion with the global corporate head, if you prefer."

Your remark forces him to sit upright and enter into work mode, but you don't miss the annoyance his glance holds and the way he grinds his jaw at your stoicism.

"Alright, Iré. I'll speak to you later." His tone is dismissive and you use that opportunity as your cue to leave his office.

As you victoriously - yet lividly - trudge down the hallway, dull excitement coursing through your veins at the thought that you've yet again escaped the impropriety that defined Mr Akinfewa, you bump into Greg, a Senior Associate in the Litigation department.

"Fine, girl! How far now?" he piques up, stopping

your movement with his right hand. "This one that you're walking away angrily. I hope we're safe," he teases.

"Morning Greg, I dey *o*, how was your weekend?"

He eyes you with his side-eye, perhaps in wonder at your odd, unenthusiastic response, before continuing, "It wasn't too bad." He nods in the direction of where he knows you're coming from, "You're coming from your boss' office?"

"Yes, *o*. That man will not kill me in this place!" Once again, you're certain that this is the only mission for the men in Lagos where you're concerned.

He watches your unease cautiously for what feels like aeons before speaking up. "I've always wanted to ask *sef*, what's going on with you and your boss?"

"What do you mean?" This catches your interest because it is not the first time someone has attempted to lay such assertions against you.

"Not to sound like a stalker or anything, but I've noticed that every morning when you get in, the first place you go to is his office. Every single morning. Without fail. I'm not implying anything *o*." He quickly defends himself, most likely picking up the quizzical expression you wear, as he continues, "But even you have to admit…it's a bit suspicious. And then with how quick you were to get promoted once he made Partner. Especially with how young you are and everything. Again, I'm not implying anything. I'm simply observing."

"Everything?"

"You know now… you're the only female SA in your department. And then the way you guys are awfully close. You're a smart girl, Iré, so don't pretend you don't know what I—people are hinting at." He almost sounds apologetic, but at the same time, his tone holds some degree of desperation for confirmation of the accusation he has levied against you.

You finally respond, your voice laced with all the coldness and rage you feel.

"You've already made your own assumption, so why bother asking me?"

His only saving grace from the ire you're justified in throwing back was the loud ringing of your phone in your hands.

"Believe what you want," is all you say, answering the phone call while stalking away angrily.

You don't remember who called or what they must have called about. You don't even remember what you said throughout the phone call. All you know is in this moment, anger violently coloured your vision. Your blood boils ten times over as you ruminate over Greg's words, emotionally oscillating between anger, frustration, pity, and disgust, finally settling on resignation.

You'd seen the signs that he was that type of man—the type that targeted the insecurities of another person, you in this scenario, by wanting to make you feel less of yourself because of your femininity—but you'd blindly ignored them, favouring your friendship with him over any glaring arrogance you saw in him.

You knew that if it had been a man who was in the exact position you were in - young and senior associate - this conversation would never have been had. Greg was merely five years older and already a senior associate like you - perhaps this gave you a license, like him, to call him a male *ashewo* because of his position and closeness with his female boss.

Once again, you're reminded that no one will ever

assume you'd made it this far with your merit as the sole reason. Greg had attempted to make you feel the one thing you'd sworn that no man would make you feel: unworthy and less, and it was a feat you did not take lightly. You didn't choose who or what you'd be born as, but you'd ensured that your life could eventually turn into one you'd be confident living and living in.

Sighing, you continue the arduous journey back to your office, your mood sour and a reminder of the desperate need to begin a soft escape plan from *Steinhart & Grey LLP.*

1:00 pm
"With all due respect, Iré, I won't take that from you," Michael shouts coldly, the bass in his voice even more pronounced, forcing you to pause from redlining the talent agreement in front of you and pay him the attention he so desperately craved from where he's stood by my door.

"Excuse me?"

You know that whenever people start sentences with '*with all due respect,*' there is usually no modicum of respect in whatever they want to say, and this is the exact situation that plays out now.

He shuts the door this time, rising to his full height, perhaps from the growing confidence he thinks his words give him. "I said I'm not going to take that from you, Iré."

Of all the Junior Associates in the corporate department - and maybe the entire firm - Michael was the one who handled the rather excruciating task of throwing you the most disrespect. You'd always been a firm believer in respect being earned by respecting others, especially in the workplace—not forcing anyone to cower in fear at your presence in some misguided belief of what respect was. You hated the eye-service respect co-workers doled on *higher-ups* who were virtually within the same age group as they were by throwing pretentious prefixes of *Ma* or *Sirs* or - God forbid - *Oga.*

Because of this, you calmly reminded anyone who attempted to bestow you with this title to simply call you Iré, the name you graced God's green earth with. However, Michael was proudly different. It had taken him over a year to even call you by your first name—in the past, he had fondly referred to you as 'her', 'she', or your personal favourite, *'that girl.'* Those were the early signs of his chauvinism. He would always wrap it up nicely for you, though, as if speaking from a place of concern, but you saw behind his facade all the time and decidedly kept mum, not saying a word to stoke his already fragile ego, which irked him all the more.

Michael had sent over his final draft of a representation agreement between the media agency the firm represented and the upcoming artiste they'd wanted to sign, which you'd thoroughly gone over only to be greeted with a mountain of mistakes not reasonably expected from a two-year PQE associate, talk less of a nearly four-year PQE associate that Michael was. You'd questioned his confidence in wanting to send it off to the client as a final draft, calling him out on the fact that it was not his first time producing substandard work and wanting to pass it off as perfection.

"Why do you feel the need to speak to me like a child?" he continues, mere moments away from throwing a tantrum, his words drawing you back to the present. "We're in the office, for god's sake. Respect me as your colleague."

Your hands freeze on the keyboard as you ready yourself to engage him in what feels like a staring contest for a long while. Before the next round of words leaves your mouth, you cheekily ask the Holy Spirit to caution your tongue, fearing that whatever unguided words come out of your mouth will force a tense meeting with HR.

"Michael? I respect you. As my colleague and as someone older than me. However, I can't say the same for you."

"What's that supposed to mean?" He clenches his hand into a fist as his face scrunches up in rage.

Your mind runs back to an unfortunate conversation you'd overheard with him and Gbenga, a paralegal in the litigation department where Michael had once again revealed how deep his misogyny and perhaps hatred of you ran. Michael was a strong believer that you did not deserve the position as a Senior - more specifically as his Senior - simply because your *'feminity' could not handle such a role,'* his words, not yours or even Gbenga's.

"She's not even up to my mother's last born, that girl," He'd gone on venomously, unbothered by the fact that he was merely five steps from your open door. "How dare she talk to me like that! As if we're mates! I'm five years older than her o! Can't she show me some respect?"

"You're talking about respect as if it's what they'll use to pay you," Gbenga had teased. "But Oga Mike, are you angry that those instructions were given to you? Abi, is it because a woman gave you those

instructions?"

"I don't care! She should know her place! Listen, I have her type at home o! And ideally, that's even where she should belong! If not for this stupid, woke Twitter generation, we wouldn't be seeing all these weak, overbearing and insecure women in positions that should ordinarily belong to men! You know say I dey talk truth." He'd laughed scornfully. "Maybe that's why she's not even married yet; because God knows her husband will suffer because of how overbearing she is! Women like her? They were made to oppress men!"

You'd loved the next statement Gbenga made that not only shut Michael up but ended that conversation:

"And that reasoning, Oga Mike, is why men like you will remain in lower positions like you are now and why women like her would keep remaining in top positions over men like you," Gbenga had scolded, his voice clearly on the edge of disgust and irritation as he'd walked away.

Gbenga, from that day on easily became your favourite male colleague at the office.

You lean back in your chair, his loud huff and shuffling feet reminding you he is still in your office, towering over your desk, disapproval wafting around his stance.

"It means, Mr Michael Esan, that I know you don't respect me. And the good thing is that I don't even need your respect; you can choke on it for all I care. The most important thing for me is that you respect your clients; respect the money that they've given us with the expectation that we produce quality for them.

And what you sent to me '*for my perusal*,' as you called it in the email you sent? It's lower than even the average standard. It's haphazardly done at best. Our clients pay us for quality, not to stroke your ego."

You roll your chair forward, turning your head back to the Mac desktop you'd been working on before he graced you with his presence.

"I expect you to take my corrections into account and submit a much better draft before the close of business tomorrow, Michael, seeing as it's an urgent document for our client."

Without looking up, you hear him fuming for what feels like ages until you hear the sharp slam of the glass door. You finally look up at his exit, thankful that the slam was not enough to shatter your door. Sighing, you glance at your watch, realising your lunch break is nearly over.

God give you strength because not only had he taken valuable time that I could have used to work on something else away, but he'd also almost effectively ruined the rest of your day.

Again, just another day at work suffering at the hands of chauvinism for the minuscule offence of feminine assertiveness.

3:30 pm
"*Ómò see nyash* o....na the only thing *wey* she *fit* give this man, nothing you *wan* tell me," The idle male hair stylist tells his fellow pedicurist as they laugh heartily and increase the volume from the overhead salon TV.

You can't help the disgust that creeps up your face, which you quickly conceal when the stylist's eyes coyly meet yours in the mirror in front of you because of how appalling and baffling the conversation is. After the altercation with Michael, you'd decided to continue working from home for the rest of the day, lest others come forward to lay dispersions of their grievances about the fact that you were a young single woman occupying a position they didn't think you deserved. Before finally heading home to wash away the insults you'd received throughout the day under the heated sprays of your overhead shower with the perfect water pressure, you'd decided to take a detour to the salon to get your hair treated and pampered—your impromptu self-care gift for fulfilling the rather gruesome obligation as one of God's strongest soldier once again.

Their conversation had started with objectifying this woman before they went on to highlight the importance of physical assets for a woman to secure the attraction of a man. They now speak at length about how a woman should be lucky and grateful and happy that a man wants her, how a woman amounts to nothing if she's not wanted by a man, essentially concluding that men define women. You realise that it is this same thought process that plagues many of the older male generations—this concept that without a man, a woman is nothing, regardless of whatever accomplishments she's achieved - that respect afforded to the woman in African society still appears to be a utopian idea.

It is more than evident, even in this conversation, that it seems inoffensive to the simple ears. In less than ten minutes, they've stripped this woman of her intelligence, work ethic and personality down to an object constituting only breasts and buttocks. The ease at which Nigerian men objectify women again speaks to the unfortunate patriarchal structures that continue to rule society. Perhaps you are also part of society's problem because you refuse to once again ruin your day by confronting and engaging them, so you plug your ears and ignore them until they finish your hair.

"Aunty, this your hair is fine *o*. It fit you *baje baje*," He smiles excitedly at you, gingerly removing the towel around your shoulder and discards it in the basket opposite him, ending its use for the day. You notice how his eyes linger on your body for a while before he finally looks back up.

You smile like there's nothing wrong and ask, "How much is my money?"

5:45 pm
"Weekend shopping already?" A deep voice murmurs behind you, the bass in his voice deliciously raising the hair on your arms as your stomach curls from desire. Your reaction is, unfortunately, normal, as you'd always been a sucker for velvety deep masculine voices. You turn sharply, noticing how wildly tall he is—a rare occurrence to meet a guy much taller than your five-foot-nine in Lagos.

After a moment's silence borne from your blatant appreciation of his physique, you laugh softly at his assumption, blushing as you look down at the packs of Red Bull, biscuits and chocolate bars you'd loaded onto your cart. "It's been a long day."

"I can imagine." His eyes twinkle with laughter as he nudges you to move forward. "Living in this Lagos alone can frustrate the hell out of you."

"*Omo*...Lagos is *definitely* not for the weak." You agree softly, your weak attempt to make small conversation with him as you wait in the queue right before the cashier calls out your turn.

"Let me help you with that," he states, immediately moving ahead of you and offloading the items from the trolley onto the conveyor. For the first time in a long time, you actively consider flirting loudly with this man before you—your subconscious desire to finally give your mother and aunt what they craved.

"Thank you," you smile softly, watching him remove each item from the trolley, banishing any feeling of dependency as he carries out this seemingly mundane task.

"I'm Iré." You finally offer some sort of compensation for the task he's taken the liberty to handle.

He smiles at me as he stretches his hand out, prompting you to shake it. "Tsemaye."

You step out together after paying for your items, almost looking like you came in together because of how easy your camaraderie is. Once we reach the parking lot, he turns and asks, "I can drop you off if you don't mind?"

"Um…." You're about to answer when he makes a salty comment beside you, immediately frustrating your interest in a further conversation with him, a comment borne in response to your mutual observation of the woman in the *Range Rover* in front of you as she zooms past whilst blasting loud music from her car.

"She's definitely doing *runs* or has a sugar daddy somewhere," he mutters as his face contours in disgust.

You pause and scrunch your face in confusion. *Not again.* "I don't get. Do you have a personal relationship with her?"

He turns to you, ridiculous confusion lining his expression. You wonder whether he really is clueless or thinks *you* are. "No?"

"Okay, then, do you at least know her? Have you guys had at least one conversation today or sometime in the past?"

"Umm...No?"

You sigh resignedly, annoyed that, *yet again,* life has thrown you into the hands of another misogynist. Console yourself that your reaction is warranted because he'd by himself chosen to reveal his true colours. "So what makes you think that she's doing *runs* or has a sugar daddy?"

He rolls his eyes and then proceeds to speak to you like a petulant child who refuses to accept an *I said so* as enough explanation to do a thing. "Iré, young lady, don't take this the wrong way or anything, but most women in this generation are lazy. They hate working for their own money, so they'd rather open their legs and earn their wages from doing that. And let's be honest, what young woman in this country earns that much that she could afford a *Range*?" His expression is as though he waits for you to confirm the nonsense he's just said.

Firstly, when people say, 'Don't take this the wrong way,' they already know that what they're going to say is derogatory or insulting, so I ask myself, 'Why bother saying what you want to say?' But that's an aside. You turn to face him fully, gathering the items in your hand. "The way you're dressed, I could easily have concluded that you're a yahoo boy."

"But I'm not—" He cuts in vehemently, almost raging because of your assumption. He scoffs at the weight and audacity of your assertion before responding in a demeaning manner, "I work a legitimate job as an Analyst at Goldman Sachs."

You shrug, matching the nonchalant way he'd cast

his accusation on the poor woman.

"In my mind, you are. I mean, those shoes scream Yahoo boy to me."

You both comically look down at his puma slides – which he's worn with a pair of red socks.

"But I wouldn't immediately jump to conclusions to assume that you are because I don't know you! It's not every guy who wears Puma slides that are Yahoo boys, same as it's not every woman who drives big cars that are *runs* babes or have sugar daddies. Like you've said about yourself, some of them work legitimate jobs. For instance, if you look in front of you, you'll see my *own* car, a result of years of saving as a Senior Associate at *Steinhart & Grey*."

I watch his eyebrows rise in shock and awe. Maybe in recognition of the firm name I'd intentionally dropped. You do not make these statements out of pride but rather a concern for his destructive mindset and the need to clarify his ridiculous opinion that legitimate success amongst women in this generation is 'uncommon.'

"Goodbye, Mr Puma," You finally conclude, rolling your eyes, leaving him standing with what now appears to be deflation – ego delicately tucked away – as he hangs his head from the embarrassment of being put in his place.

Same day, same *wahala*.

It was, unfortunately, the same script you were constantly rinsing and repeating daily that forced you to the conclusion: that Lagos men were unrepentantly after your life for your simple crime of remaining single and being arrogantly unbothered by your perpetual singleness.

OLUWABUNMI ADARAMOLA leads a dual life, balancing academia during the day with her vibrant imagination at night. To refine her writing skills, she dedicated herself to online courses, completing programs at Wesleyan University and Michigan State University. Her short story, Palmwine Promises, was featured in Brittle Paper's prestigious 2023 Festive Anthology.

Additionally, her works have been published in renowned platforms like The Three Boats Magazine, The Kalahari Review, and The African Writer, with forthcoming contributions to The Sprinng Literary Magazine. Aside from writing, Oluwabunmi indulges in her love for coffee and cheesy romance novels, showcasing her passion for storytelling and literature.

SOLVED

- Pearl Adjavon

The Harmattan wind cut through the hush reverence that cloaked the land, portending a noisy ruffle of withered plantain leaves and a dance of swirling dust. Their eyes burned. Appiah could taste the blood in the mucus he'd just sucked down from his nose, and Salisu could feel the skin atop his lower lip flake off like old paint. Their brown skins shone white with dryness as they lay stretched over the ground, fingers caked with dirt. Salisu made his first move, gathering and releasing kernels into pits. Appiah played next…

"Good game, man!" Appiah expressed, pumping his friend-opponent's hand.

"Good for me, you mean." Salisu laughed. "I finished you!"

"I concur," Appiah replied in good humour. "A game of ball is *my* ball game, pun intended."

Salisu shook his head. "Man, what the heck is 'pun'?"

"You don't know? Well! That's why I insist you return to school. You are becoming dumb!"

"Shut it, Ape," Salisu sniggered heedlessly, musing on the thrill the local board game brought him. He recalled with bittersweet relish the warm nights he had spent with his father inside their study. For hours on end, the two would tire their knuckles over rounds of Oware until the spying moon itself pleaded exhaustion. Evenings to come were destined to be the most exhilarating, yet Selah and her mother had not barged in on their lives. Salisu felt a gnawing ache in his heart.

"You know I can't. Oware means too much to me; It wants all of me, bro."

"C'mon, your parents need to know you are alive, at least."

"My father won't give a hoot, and I don't care for - . Just keep your mouth shut!"

The boys stayed for another round of the game, adjusting only their body posture to make for comfort as they dropped and clawed palm kernels out of holes they had dug in the ground.

Later that night, Salisu sauntered to the market centre, wondering at his friend's sudden use of big grammar. Salisu had only been out of school for eight weeks, but it seemed Appiah had gotten a year's worth of lessons in his absence; Appiah did not use to be that good at Oware either. All Appiah knew, Salisu had taught him, or at least that was what Salisu believed.

The next time the two met was three days later, after the Harmattan haze had subsided. The old pits had almost been covered up by dust. The boys didn't possess an actual board with pebbles as Oware demanded, so they dug small pits into the ground and used palm kernels instead. They dug out all twelve with

KEPRESSNG

their blanched fingers and filled each one with four kernels. This time, they barricaded their nasals and buccals with bandanas they tied behind their ears.

Salisu played first. The pits were called houses, and the kernels were their occupants. The houses were split into a pair of six rows, one for each player. To win, a player had to capture a higher number of kernels in the end. Salisu grabbed kernels from a house on his side, dropping one after the other as he moved from house to house in a counterclockwise direction until all four were gone. Appiah played next, drawing his kernels and dropping his last in a house that had only one. He made his first capture there, earning the two kernels. Salisu shifted slightly, eyeing his opponent's win in denial before hastily executing his move. Appiah, however, played meticulously, patiently observing before taking his turn with calculated precision.

"Well, that was a silly move," said a voice to Salisu after he had dropped his final kernel; Appiah, by playing with the strategy of a cat stalking a mouse, had won.

"You should've counted them first!" the chiding voice continued, drawing closer.

Stunned by his unexpected defeat, Salisu quietly replaced all the kernels. "Rematch!" he ordered cooly. By now, the bearer of the voice had crept up to them unnoticed, planting herself noiselessly beside the boys, equally drawn into the game. It was a tight match. Appiah's slow and steady actions were countered by Salisu's sudden and jerky ones. At the end of the second game, it was a slight win for the latter: twenty-three against twenty-five.

Appiah's usual 'Good game, man.' was met with a mortal glare from Salisu.

"You played like a chicken," Salisu taunted with

false bravado.

"Quite the opposite!" a voice mumbled softly.

The boys only then seemed to notice the girl who sat cross-legged beside them.

"You were both quite predictable, but you," she pointed at Salisu, "What was that? Your play was so inept."

It was like a slap to his face. Indignant, Salisu glowered at her. "What do you know?"

"I've played before," she countered imperiously. "It's easy if you can solve it."

"Solve it?" Appiah asked, intrigued. "What do you mean?"

"Oware is a solved game. What? It's true! If you can solve it, you can beat any player." The girl stood. "My name is Ama."

"Appiah. Th-th-that's mine," the boy stuttered, rubbing his hardened palm against the gentle creases of hers.

Salisu was having none of it. With a sombre hush, he gathered his kernels into his pockets and rose to leave. "Meet me here next Friday, Ape. As for you -" he said, gesturing toward the girl. "Take your lies away with you and mind your own business." He stomped off.

Salisu tried hard to quell his anger and forget those comments - 'predictable', 'inept', 'solved'. He'd lost himself in thought and had almost been run over. The cart he'd been pushing around the market since he arrived there had been the one to receive the full blow of the speeding truck. He'd been beaten, insulted, and spat on. The station master had smacked his face and prayed for thunder to strike his pathetic little frame down. Now, without the few pesewas he could live on, he turned to theft by smuggling food from careless victims till he could find someone to employ him.

It was late when he crawled into a ball in front of a kiosk with others and had nowhere else to spend the night. As he twisted and turned on the cold, hard pavement, he felt warm moisture trickle deliciously up his thigh and shorts. He dropped his hand into the warmth and brought it up to his nose.

Urine!

"Ugh?!" he yelped, shaking himself off the floor.

A wide-eyed toddler stared down at him, naked and picking her nose.

Appalled, he bolted off, raining crude jibes on the unsuspecting mother. He strolled through the dreary streets of Makola. It was dark, and the market centre was almost asleep. The stubborn vendors still advertising their wares were simply begging for trouble from the likes of him.

Offei had taught him to steal smart: a little at a time. That was more sustainable and forgivable. So, when the kebab stand had gathered enough crowd, he forced his way through and slid a skewer out unnoticed. Never mind that the meat was still raw. He bit into it and searched for a place to sleep, somewhere uninfected by teenage mothers and their peeing chits.

As he wandered through a dimly lit alleyway, his ears began to tingle at the unmistakable sound of pebbles hitting boards. He followed the melody like a lifeline, his ears twitching and whispering to him to pass here and then there. They didn't drag him on too long, for soon, he stood before the entrance of a clandestine tavern nestled between towering buildings that seemed to lean in with an interest that matched his own. The sound of pebbles cascading over boards like raindrops on a tin roof echoed against the alley walls, drugging him.

He crossed the narrow passageway, bathed in the blueish-red glow of flickering bulbs, and pushed against the heavy wooden door. Soft melodic strains of Highlife music washed over him, carrying with it a strong fetidness of beer and smoke that nearly choked him senseless. A motley crew of the market's hustlers seeking respite from life's chaos was slumped over worn wooden tables laden with shiny boards and bottles of beer. Salisu stared hungrily.

"Hey!" a stoic figure hollered, staggering over. "You play, boy? Yes? You are really good? Okay. Five cedis to enter. What? No money?"

Salisu was shoved out as quickly as he had entered. Unfazed, he returned the next day. And the day after. Peeping through the windows and catching glimpses of the convivial atmosphere within. The *Night Soul* was a beacon of warmth and camaraderie to weary men who had worked themselves lifeless in the outside world. Here, their souls were restored. They played against each other; their laughter and chatter mingled with the pelting ta-ta-ta rhythm of dancing pebbles. The winners amongst them played with the champion of the game, Toby Willis. Toby, Salisu discovered, was a Jamaican Rastafarian who was reputed to have *solved* the game.

Toby bore a severe figure that humbled most men at the bar. He stood taller than all from the shoulder up and wore dreadlocks as dense as an evil forest. He spoke little and always sat in a shadowy corner, nursing a drink and silently observing the nocturnal face-offs before him. His standoffishness made him an odium to the rest of the players, and yet, try as they might, no one could beat him! Old men of acclaim came to play against him and lost. People who claimed to be family with the game, from the Mancala family, could hardly match his skill.

Toby had truly *solved* the game. That word again! Salisu wondered how anyone could solve Oware. He thought again about Ama's comment. If it was true that the game could be solved, he had to learn how and challenge the likes of Toby.

"Phew! You stink!" Ama grimaced with a pinch of her nose.
Salisu felt quite slovenly with his tattered garments oozing off a foul stench and his unkempt hair knotting unattractively into small clusters atop his head. The two pairs of eyes stared disapprovingly at him. He'd wanted to chide Appiah for bringing that worm along, but his shame kept him mute.

"Don't you shower?" Ama persisted.

"Don't ask stupid questions!" he warned. "Let's play, Ape!" Salisu hesitated as he gathered and planted kernels in the pits. Appiah played with a confidence that further unnerved his opponent. With great uneasiness, Salisu kept playing into the hands of Appiah, who revelled in delight with each capture.

"Hey, you can't do that!" Salisu attacked.

"Yes, I can. You've given me a second kernel in my house, and you've still got one in your hand, Sal. Drop it," Appiah defended, pointing to an empty house. "It belongs there!"

"Damn it!" Salisu hurled the last kernel into the designated pit. He picked at his blistered lip in frustration. He'd just lost to Appiah by an embarrassing lot.

"You know, It's really easy if you can solve it," Ama opined in response when Salisu howled in agony.

"Shut up! I don't need you! I don't need any of you!" Salisu barked. "You cheated!" he accused. "Don't think you won! Get out of here!" With this, he got up and threw his kernels at them.

"Hey man, chill," Appiah reasoned. "It's just a game."

"Is that so, Ape? You think it's just a game? This is my life!"

"Look man, I'm telling your parents your whereabouts. You need help."

Salisu hit him in the face.

As the night wore on, the treacherous sun stole itself away again, leaving Salisu to the mercy of the dark and frigid night. He crawled his way around the pits, feeling for the lost kernels strewn about the grass. In his hasty desperation, he grazed his bare knee against a sharp stone, sending a stinging pain up his leg. *This was hopeless,* he cried, drowning himself in a fresh wave of tears. He could remember clearly the route back home to good food and a warm bed, but his father wouldn't accept him now, not after all that had happened. He'd chosen to leave rather than stay and worship Selah's mother the way his father had.

"You shouldn't live like this," Ama uttered some feet away, startling him.

"Go away!" Salisu growled. He spat on his finger and dabbed his sore lips.

Ama crouched beside him in the prickly grass and attempted to nurse his cut.

"Why did you run away from home?" Ama asked

brokenly. He cast her a suspicious eye. "Appiah told me," Ama explained. "Surely it wasn't just to play Oware, right?"

"And if it were?"

"Then I'd say you were possessed by a demon," she replied with a soft chuckle.

Annoyed, Salisu tried rising to his feet.

"Go home," he repeated. "What do you want here in the dark anyway? Oh, do your parents no longer want you?" he asked with a wicked grin.

Ama gasped, cut by his rudeness. "I care for you," she said cautiously. "And I want to help you."

She dropped Vaseline on the finger with the saliva, and reluctantly, he ran that on his raw lip instead. She gazed into his pained eyes laden with many more tears unshed. She wished to draw him out and comfort him, know all the whys, but he was more distant than a hundred miles could put between two human beings.

"How do you solve the game?" Salisu asked after a long pause.

Ama thought a while before speaking, "You have to calculate it, Salisu. You need to know a lot of Maths."

"Offei, teach me maths." Salisu inched his face closer to his drunk brother's the next afternoon, poking him awake.

"What for? So you could rob me, Fox? Ha!"

"No, brother," he sighed. "I want, no, I need maths to solve Oware. I'm going to be a champion, like Toby Willis."

Offei sat up for a moment and seemed to be considering the words when he erupted into thunderous laughter. "Stupid boy! Here! Beer should give you some sense."

"Please, Offei."

"Hey, That game is for fools who have enough life, money, and time to waste." He grabbed Salisu by the collar. "You have nothing! Think about how to survive, boy... and besides," he added with a coy smirk, "my maths master died years ago. Ha!"

The intoxicated Offei swooned to the ground. Salisu gathered him up and threw him onto a nearby bench. He studied the inert bony frame with anger and pity. Offei was only seventeen, and Salisu was fourteen. Salisu thought Offei a fool sometimes for drinking himself into a stupor. Offei could do no work till he was sober, and when he finally was, he'd crumple with hunger and steal like a fool, nothing like what he had taught Salisu. He would get caught on countless occasions for shoplifting. Many times, Salisu had to share his money with Offei after dragging him out of the gutters where his apprehenders would beat and leave him. But Offei often watched Salisu's back, too, like the day he'd broken his cart. Offei had fought the truck driver off. He had some good in him, and Salisu had long since entertained the audacious idea that he and Offei were brothers and street brothers.

Friday afternoon rolled in again, but Salisu didn't go meet Appiah for a match like always. Offei was at it again so Salisu could borrow and push the second cart around the market, carrying customers' loads for them until Offei was sober. He'd been able to make four-forty cedis so far. Sixty more pesewas and Salisu would have enough to play at *Night Soul*.

Retiring after hard work, he slithered through the narrow streets to the alleyway. It was just after dusk, so the bar was nearly empty. Salisu stared longingly through the windows at the shiny brown boards and pebbles spread neatly across the tables. How polished they looked! He could kiss each pebble good night every day for the rest of his life. His breath stained the glass, drawing him out of his reverie. Sixty more pesewas. He leapt away from the window and dashed back into the main street. Some buyers could still be spotted around.

"Madam, I can carry the goods for you," Salisu offered, snatching the polythene bag from a woman's hand before she could protest. She slapped him, for she mistook him for a thief. Salisu couldn't blame her. He looked the part. Despair stole over him when she yanked her bag back and walked away, pushing him aside. He, however, persisted and resumed his search for the next potential client.

An elderly woman with an angry pout was beckoning a *kaya*-girl, a female head porter, to help her carry her large sack. Salisu followed the elderly woman's gaze. Ugh! It was the girl with the little piddler. Salisu outran her and heaved his client's burden onto his head. As he adjusted the load, he thought his neck would sink into his chest! The weight tipped precariously in every direction.

Alarmed, the *kaya*-girl's angry features instantly lit up with relief and naughty amusement. She eyed him saucily before turning away. Salisu struggled to keep up with his client. She had swift feet for such an old lady, but he couldn't blame her either. The likes of him were out and about, set loose by the encroaching darkness. They were the market's vampires, those thieves, and they drained hard and fast. Tonight, Salisu could not let that happen to his customer, especially not when his game depended so much on it. With this resolve, he quickened his steps, willing his head to cease wobbling.

"Fifty pesewas, ma'am," Salisu charged, rubbing his aching neck. He'd let down the woman's sack into the trunk of a bus. It started to move.

"No. Too much! Forty."

"Okay," Salisu agreed desperately when the bus began to pick up speed. The elderly woman flung the coins out of the speeding vehicle, sending them flying in all directions. Salisu caught only one - a ten pesewa coin. The rest treacherously disappeared into the shadows. It didn't take long for him to realise that all of them had instantly been abducted by the avaricious creeps lurking around. He sprung into corners and slid between walls, tossing and turning here and there, but who was he kidding? Tonight, the vampires had drunk *his* blood, only that he could not die out of his misery. He could only cry.

Salisu woke up the next morning to the ear-splitting noise of hopeless peddlers fraying their vocal cords to stay alive. He was lying by a fishmonger's stall, and the owner was shooing him away.

Salisu moved away with a neck as stiff as a poker to the bus station.

"Where have you been, Fox?" Offei asked upon seeing Salisu.

"Working," Salisu answered tersely.

"Good, boy! Take this. It's bread and butter. You finish that! Well, gotta go. Watch yourself, boy. These fools here are wolfish."

Salisu shielded his food from the other cart-pushers.

KEPRESSNG

He wondered at Offei's sudden show of concern. Normally, he would have asked Salisu about the money he'd made from work and then take half of it. Salisu let out a breath he didn't know he'd been holding. The bread was fresh, hot even, and the butter had melted into it. Salisu nibbled at it and hid the rest, saving it for later. He climbed under a shed somewhere and slept his exhaustion away till he felt a sharp prick on his thigh.

"Get up, Fox. Eat." It was dusk, and Offei handed him a full skewer of hot sausage kebab, which was well-cooked.

Salisu gasped. "That's expensive! One whole cedi! Where did you get the money from?"

"My money, my problem. Eat."

Salisu ate half of it and shoved the rest into his pocket with his almost stale piece of bread.

"You don't need to work tonight, Fox. It's Saturday. Rather, go to Mosé's bus and count the number of seats in it." Offei said, replacing Salisu on the mat. Salisu gazed at the still bony frame in confusion. Offer's breath did smell of alcohol, but he wasn't drunk, and it relieved Salisu in no small way. He went to do as he'd been told. Offei was good. The station master made him do all the ciphering whenever his calculator conked out, which was almost always. Offei, through that, had gained the respect of the other boys, and they refrained from harassing Salisu for fear of him. Salisu was proud to call Offei his brother. His street brother.

"How many?" Offei asked when Salisu returned.

"Fifteen."

"So, how many passengers?"

"Fifteen!" came the pompous reply.

"Idiot!" Offei smacked the back of his student's

head. "I said, passengers! If the driver takes a seat and the conductor takes another…"

"Oh, twelve, twelve," Salisu corrected sheepishly.

"And if each one paid forty p, how much would you earn at the end of one trip?"

Salisu grimaced. "Offei, this is hard."

Salisu spent the rest of the afternoon reciting the twelve times table under Offei's keen watch. A slip-up earned Salisu a sharp smack on his occiput. Later, Offei grabbed a rock and drew twelve circles on the pavement. Salisu could only produce twenty-five out of the forty-eight kernels from his pockets. He ran and collected twenty-three stone chips from a heap beside an ongoing building.

Offei picked a random house and sowed along. "What can you see?" He asked Salisu, studying him.

"You have an empty house." he shrugged offhandedly, extending his hand to play. Offei slapped it off.

"Now, what can you foresee?"

Salisu sat back, confused. "I foresee myself winning," he grinned.

"Idiot! Look. If you grab from this house, you will drop a seed in this empty house of mine, which I can easily capture, but grab from there," Offei pointed in another direction. "And you will be forcing me to empty all my houses so you can make easy captures for yourself. Think and count!"

Salisu learnt to count before carrying pieces from any house. Offei told him to combine knowledge with skill to understand the game's complexity.

"Just tell me how to solve it," Salisu said in frustration after losing to Offei the third time.

"Ha! There is no solution to it. Flawless calculation,

that's all it is!"

Salisu doubted. "But you have solved it. So has Appiah and Toby Willis."

Offei shot him a look of apprehension. "Look, I don't know who Appiah is, but my father has sure not solved anything."

"Your father!?"

Later that night, Salisu went to the bar to watch them play. With an ever-increasing intrigue, he studied how they played, wondering what move he would have made had he been this player or that. That night, he would have his very first clear glimpse of Toby Willis. Had what Offei said been true? The man's face could hardly be made out, with his thick sideburns and long moustache invading every inch of his face.

"Terrifying, hmm?" a boy remarked.

Salisu turned to find Offei standing next to him and bearing a cool expression.

"This is what he left me for?"

Salisu laughed in disbelief. "So, you're Jamaican?"

Offei's nostrils flared, "You nuh believe me, bredren? Maybe yuh should guh back a yuh school and get a propa education so yuh can use some common sense. Look yah now, blind youth. Mi hair deh inna cornrow, an' everybody rate mi. Why yuh tink dat?"

"You are smart," Salisu rationalised. "People naturally respect that."

"No, bredren, it nuh go so. Mi fada come yah when Mama dead. Him did mash up, never like look pon me 'cause mi favor her. Him gi mi to di station master fi tek care a mi. Him send money come gi mi. Mi drink beer wid it till yuh come. Now mi haffi tek care a yuh. Yuh a mi bredda."

The boys entered *Night Soul* the following day.

KEPRESSNG

They were shown a table and asked to wait. Salisu sank into the foamy seat, savouring every inch of it. He touched the worn table everywhere his eye could reach and finally rested in hand on the board. The temptation to lean down and kiss the polished surface was too strong. He'd not touched a real one for so long that he almost forgot what it was like. He fished out some smooth, shiny pebbles and rubbed them gently in his palm, groaning pleasantly at their feel.

Offei chuckled at his street brother's obvious affection for the game. He stared at the weathered stone walls adorned with vintage posters and old photographs of stories long forgotten. He remembered many of them. He shifted uncomfortably when his father entered. He bowed his face so that Toby wouldn't see him. Daddy Lumba's *Ankwanoma* played as the games were beginning. Toby sat in his corner, nose deep into a book as the games began. He usually did so to discourage any disturbance, not that he could even see the pages anyway.

The pairing began.

Salisu found the men easy to beat. They played just for fun, drinking beer and making confused moves. Salisu was at a great advantage, playing with a clear head and being grateful for not getting hooked on beer. Offei played intently, selecting the moves that offered the greatest advantages in the long run. The atmosphere became more intense as the night wore on, and the boys kept outing the usual players.

They were now on to the mid-level. Salisu began to make heady moves out of sheer excitement. Offei shot him an 'I'll smack your head if you are not careful' look. Salisu could not tell who or what his next opponent was. Mostly, they were either bus drivers, mongers, or the regular, distinct ones in the mix. A red nose pointed out from under a black Bowler hat. Messy eyebrows shrouded his eyes, making them look like hollow pots. His fingers were white and wrinkled. He played very silently, seemingly unaware of the other men cheering him on. Shaken, Salisu played hard and fast, feigning confidence and playing nothing like how Offei had instructed earlier. He moved thoughtlessly, and soon, his houses were empty. His opponent's lined face crinkled into a gloating smile as he stood up and moved to the next challenger. Salisu was out. Offei pulled him aside.

"Man, what was that?" Offei asked.

"I wasn't thinking," Salisu replied mournfully.

"Obviously! That was Fitzroy, Rupert Fitzroy. He's an Englishman settled in Ghana. A professor. He studies the game like a deranged man. The only one who beats him is Toby."

"I could have defeated him had I been careful."

"Maybe."

Offei shrugged and returned to the game.

Now, many were out and, on the sidelines, cheering on and heckling away at each other, and Offei made it to the final stage. His opponent was a bald man draped in a rich Kente cloth, and as though that were not telling enough, he was further accessorised with ornaments made of pure gold. He drew a crowd with his cackling laughter and pompous talk. An Asante chief, no doubt. Offei knew it would not be easy to beat such a player. After a protracted match, the chief was silently escorted out. No one dared to cheer when such a dignitary had lost to a street boy.

Toby stared at his son with pained recognition. He watched as Offei patiently drew the chief out of his safety net. He snickered at the chief's stricken face when the boy captured three houses.

It was now Fitzroy against Offei. Whoever won would play with Toby. Offei looked in his father's direction as the game began, but Toby masked his emotions and looked on with indifference. Incensed, Offei turned away and eyed the professor.

"Move already!" Offei yelled when the Professor had pored over the game for a while.

Salisu offered to knead Offei's tense shoulders, but Offei shrugged him off.

The professor made his first capture smoothly. Offei couldn't concentrate any longer. Upset, he shot out of his seat and bolted out the door. Once under the cool night sky, He let off steam by kicking stones he found in the alleyway.

"I told the station master to put you into school," Toby said softly when he found his son.

Offei ignored him.

"Why aren't you in school?"

"I've not been to school for two years, and you notice that now?"

"Why?"

"What's it to me? You abandoned me so you could forget your pain. What do you think mine did to me? It ate me up. Two years ago was when I last saw you. I know the Master told you I left school, but did you care? No. Didn't even look for me once..." Offei broke off.

Toby gazed into the skies with regret, a constant feeling he was forcing himself to get used to now. He hardened his face against the swirling emotions arising from two years of buried pain. He knew nothing could excuse him for how he had pushed his son away.

"You'll return to school. Tell your friend there to go back home and resume school. Fitzroy will take you both to London. He's introducing the game at the English Board Game Championship and wants you boys on his team."

When Salisu received the news, he returned home, albeit with trepidation. His stepmother, Yaba, upon seeing him, gave him a lingering hug. She offered to dress him up in his finest attire to meet his father, but he refused. When Fareed, Salisu's father, returned from work hours later, he entered and cocooned himself in his study right away, completely oblivious to his son's return from the streets. Salisu emerged from his bedroom minutes later, expecting to stumble upon the uncomfortable sight of his father and stepmother caressing like they used to. Instead, he found Yaba alone on the sofa, weeping. Suddenly uncomfortable, Salisu considered retracing his steps back into his room, but Yaba noticed him and gestured for him to share the sofa with her.

"Where is my father?" Salisu asked when he finally sat.

"In there," Yaba sniffed, pointing towards the study. "He's been sleeping in there ever since you left."

Salisu stiffened. That could not possibly be true! His father had stated in no unclear terms that he would 'love nothing more than for Salisu to take his bad attitude and be gone!'

"No, no, no, my boy. He was too angry then. He didn't mean to drive you out of the house," Yaba explained tenderly, reaching for the boy's hand.

Salisu snatched it away. "You're lying! The only reason why he's shut up in there is because he's seen you for the real villain you are. You and Selah are not welcome here, so just pack up and leave!"

Yaba's flushed face crumbled with hurt. "Your dinner is on the table," she said with grave silence and departed to her room.

By morning, Salisu's anger had subsided. He quietly joined Yaba for breakfast. Thankfully, she wasn't all weepy like the previous night. Salisu was surprised she hadn't packed up and left already. When Fareed appeared from the study, Salisu sat up immediately, eyeing his father guardedly should the man lose his temper and decide to throw the radio set upon recognising Salisu. The pathetic figure his father cut was unsettling; the man had unkempt hair sticking out in bizarre directions.

Yaba squatted on her haunches in greeting Fareed, but he waved it off with some incoherent response, causing her to refocus her attention on setting the table. Selah came fluttering around her mother like some exotic bird desperate for attention. She rambled on and on about the most random topics, clearly unaffected by the uneasy atmosphere. Selah had rushed into Salisu's room the night before with her five-year-old sass and accused him of deserting her. Her insistence on sharing his bed that night for fear of the 'monsters' in her room had little accosted him to her never-ending chatter. She was beginning to frighten him with her unrelenting clinginess.

"Have some tea, Sali, please. Here, here," Selah implored frantically, inadvertently drawing Fareed's attention to his son.

Fareed was taken aback by the sight of Salisu. Dumbfounded, he gaped dubiously as though his mind were playing games with him. He disappeared into the kitchen and returned with water splashed across his weary face.

"Is it really you?" Fareed asked, his voice taut with pain. He had imagined this day so many times that he couldn't believe he was truly beholding Salisu again after all those months. He slowly advanced towards his son, who still had fear and mistrust written across his face. Fareed pulled the boy up by the shoulders and held him in an embrace.

"My boy," he cried. "My dear boy."

Gradually, Salisu's obstinacy gave in to his pent-up feelings of loneliness and dejection, and soon, he, too, was drowning in his tears. They played Oware that morning, deploying their shared love for the game as common ground to rebuild their severed relationship. Salisu gingerly related his ordeal on the streets to his father. Shifting uncomfortably from where he sat, Fareed couldn't help but concede to his role in the entire incident. His temper had gotten the best of him. Had he been less dismissive, Salisu might not have felt so utterly alone. His love for Yaba shouldn't have blinded him to his son's despair.

"I'm…I'm sorry," Fareed stammered, unsure of what else to say.

Caught off-guard by his father's use of those unfamiliar words, Salisu stared awkwardly, saying nothing.

"Perhaps, it's time for you to go back to school," Fareed gently suggested.

Salisu felt a glimmer of hope. Sensing his tongue loosening, he informed Fareed about the offer from Rupert Fitzroy.

"It'll change my life, Papa," he added ardently.

If Fareed had any doubts about the idea, they were quickly dispelled by the fervour in his son's voice. He nodded slowly, a weight seeming to lift off his shoulders.

Salisu couldn't believe it! He reached out and squeezed his father's hand, a silent gesture of forgiveness. As the morning sun flitted through the glass-paned windows, Salisu judged it an indication of better days ahead. He made a mental promise to give his stepmother and sister a chance at loving him. He knew the effort would mean a lot to his father. Their conjoined support might help him sail through the foreseeable future. And perhaps, with Offei and Rupert's guidance, he could become a champion in the world of Oware.

PEARL ADJAVON, a spirited Ghanaian graduate of Ghana National College, learned the values of perseverance and determination from her bustling household upbringing. Her devout Christian faith serves as a source of solace and strength in her pursuits.

With diverse interests, Pearl aims to pursue a dual degree in Engineering and English to become an Energy Engineer and Author. She seeks to inspire Ghanaian and African women to achieve greatness.

THE FIRST DAY TICKET

- Ayo-Daniel O. Ayodeji

The morning dew smell was sweet in the Boji farm settlement area. It was a blend of luxuriant green foliage and soil rich in plant compost over time. It had not rained for weeks, perhaps a month or two, but it dawned fresh for the break of day every morning.

Hamidu Ibrahim just rose from the bed, an improvised bamboo and flat, tatty mattress. He was a youth corper serving in the National Youth Service Corp and had been posted up north for his national assignment. He had termed the whole exercise an adventure of a year-long, and he was ready to explore every bit of it socially and responsibly, but today, he would be late to catch a train if he was not quick enough to join buses going out of Boji.

The Boroji village was one of the many clans of Boji where he was particularly living. It was the time of the year when it had a weeklong traditional ceremony that would not harbour any stranger amidst them, so he must vacate the land for at least a week. He had the choice of visiting home to see his parents and other members of his family, but that was several thousands of kilometres down in the southern part of the country.

He, however, thought visiting Salisu, his cousin in the nearby northern state, was his best bet. Salisu Ibrahim, his cousin, was not married but gainfully employed at some place he could not tell at the moment. He drove a car and lived in a tastefully furnished rented apartment. Salisu was living the dream of a Nigerian youth who had trained at university, graduated, and now earned money from the labour market. A young man who was free of marital or familial encumbrance meant they would have a good time together without being conscious of time or family responsibility after a long time they had both seen each other.

The last three months had been somewhat lonesome for Hamidu. Being a teacher in a rural community school with a diminutive population, the lowest he had ever known, he enjoyed some free time his counterparts in the city could not. He had enough time on his hands and could only put everything into reading books because he had little or no activities to invest his time. There was no internet access in Boroji.

This very morning, there were no chores to be done, as he had planned, so he rushed to brush his teeth and bathe. He put on his clothes, a shirt, and a pair of trousers, got his backpack, locked up his room and dashed out to the only bus park in Boji. It was a small one that he thought did not fit to be called so because it barely had buses ready for journeys, but this morning was also different. There were two minibuses going to town. It was already so bright, but it was just half past six in the morning by the clock image on his phone, which unstably flickered only on the lowest network bar. Simply, there was no steady network available, he assumed. It was only a matter of minutes; the bus would be in motion since it was only short of one passenger to make it full.

It was a wild calmness to be back in the city with the bustling energy of people who pushed, shoved, and avoided jumbled steps. He felt alive again with the new sunshine on every animate and inanimate object around him. Everything, even the day, was different from the usual. The city reeked of gasoline or burned out the exhaust of cars and other outsized vehicles. There were vehicles and crowds of people all about. It was the reality of modernity. Hamidu brought out his phone from his trousers pocket, which caught all the network bars. He smiled as he dialled his cousin.

"Hello," his cousin's voice on the other side sounded harsh. "You were supposed to be here yesterday."

"Hello, Salisu. I'm sorry. There was no way I could make it down yesterday, and I couldn't call either."

"And I called you all through to be sure, but your call was not going through?"

"Still so sorry, it was network issues," Hamidu replied. "But good that I will make it today."

The voice of his cousin on the other side toned up in anger.

"I will be out of town, I mean it. I'm busy today!" Salisu said. "You should know better to make appointments with consent. Wait for me at the bus park, whatever time you arrive, and please, stick close to your phone."

KEPRESSNG

The phone was suddenly dead on the other side. Hamidu was confused, but then his phone rang again, and he picked up.

"Make sure you take a bus going to Kawo motor park," Salisu's stern voice came through and dropped again, this time with some urgency. He did not wait for a reply.

"I am already at the station!" Hamidu tried to say this to still an engaged phone, but it was cut in some desperation he could not fathom. He dialled back the number, but it switched off. His confusion grew. He didn't know whether to take on the journey or not anymore. He had bought the train ticket, so he thought it was imperative to go on the journey. The train honked a few meters away; he checked his ticket. AK-49 was listed as the next in line, and it was the train in sight, so he picked up his backpack to join up.

The scenery from inside of the speed train was beautiful. It was moving on and leaving the world behind. Everything moved fast, and in a flash, hungry landscapes were left behind for richer, smoother encroachment of the topography of lands. Some faces in the coaches were unhappy; maybe from the tiredness of the protracted crossing, and few others looking so quite cheerful. Hamidu seemingly studied everything and everyone around him, in and out of the train. It was his first time on a train. He had already assumed it was a certainty: it would be a pleasurable first trip experience on a train.

The train made progressive intrusion into the early shade of nightfall as the horizon disappeared and the path of rails got dimmer to the slight evening light not very accessible. The sun was going down, and the dusty dusk was prodding its presence, but the air-conditioning facility on the train was suiting, and Hamidu continued to stare out the window of the train.

Glimmer images of three men suddenly moved past. Hamidu thought he saw them; he actually saw those figures. It was too late to catch a glimpse of them, even if he looked back from the window. He wondered what manner of men would stand close to where the train trailed rapidly, especially in a deserted area. There had been no agricultural settlement in the last thirty minutes of the journey, he had noted.

The train had barely moved for ten minutes since the last time he thought he saw shadows of men when he spotted a man with a rifle hanging from his shoulder in the company of another man. He could see they had turbans on their heads and faces covered with pieces of scarf. He could not make a thing of the repeating figures, especially now that one stippled a gun somewhere between. They were certainly not military in the way they were clothed. Hamidu could not hold it anymore. His peace was troubled.

"Please, ma'am, do you know where we are?" He turned to the lady beside him and asked. She was engrossed with her little boy, who was about two years old.

"I really don't know" she answered, "It's my first time taking a train in Nigeria". She was back to the attention of her child in another second.

"We are probably at Katari," the man next to her answered. "The axis is Katari-Rijana in Kaduna."

"Okay. Thank you" Hamidu thanked the man for the knowledge, but suddenly, his eyes caught more men with guns hanging from their necks, and he pointed to the window for them to see.

KEPRESSNG

In a moment of time, their eyes, too, caught the bewilderment of the sight of many armed men, some riding on motorcycles. While they were still toiling in incomprehension, in yet another moment that seemed all dreamingly prolonged, there was a blast with an enormous bang jolting human bodies from one point to another. A huge fireball flashed before their eyes, and everything went up in flames in a fragment of a second. The huge noise, fire and displacement all happened within the same fraction of a time. Then, a sudden halt was in motion, and the explosion grounded the train instantly. It had lost its track momentum and had derailed.

"My baby, my baby," a woman cried.

Hamidu was subconsciously hearing the voice of the lady next to him. The force of the explosion had thrown him against the wall of the coach, and he had temporarily lost consciousness. He tried to open his eyes. Everything was blurry. His vision had become foggy, and he could not tell who or what was by his side. He moved a little, with his eyes opened wider, in a struggle for better vision in the smoke. He was stumbling, but he tried getting up on his feet each time. The little bundle of weight beside him was not luggage, but the little baby had been launched in the opposite direction with the same impact as him.

He carried the baby and crawled over damaged seats to the direction of the voice; it was then he realized that the baby was not making an effortful movement, nor was he crying for pain. The mother took him from Hamidu, both looking into each other's eyes in the flashes of flames burning, in taciturnity of understanding of the state of the child. She held the boy to her chest and started sobbing uncontrollably. It was the sound of crying that brought Hamidu to the realization of other people's cries of pain.

Kra-ta-ta-ta-ta!!!!!!
Kra-ta-ta-ta-ta!!!!!!!!
Kra-ta-ta-ta-ta!!!!!!!!!!

The sound of cracks of guns filled the air. The spraying of volleys of bullets in all directions would not ensure any man's survival, he was certain. More cries filled the choking hot air. Cough and tears were common. Loud screams rented the air. Some people had been hit by bullets. Some had dropped dead next to their seat partners. Hamidu felt a sharp piercing in his body. His upper arm had been hit. He could feel the wetness of blood as his flowery white shirt was red and clingy to his fleshy arm. His blood was now flowing freely, and the pain from the hand was excruciating, almost unbearable. He grabbed and held on to his arm, probably to arrest the bleeding or assuage the pain in it. The train is under attack, he thought to himself. However, by whom, how could he know? He remembered he had read a publication in which the railway corporation stated that the train itself was bulletproof. Where was the proof that the train was?

He felt some brisk movements around him, and a strong arm pulled him up by the shoulder. He did not know if he was being saved, but his body followed the action with ease. He was being desperately led through the cramped aisle, scattered with baggage, until an opening where he was pushed out. He fell on the dusty earth, and other hands grabbed him from both sides. And he knew from the grip that they were not safe hands, and neither were they headed to safety. Immediately, he understood why bullets were flying around inside the coaches; the marauders had gained entry on the train. It was not a mere attack but an invasion, too.

Thirty minutes later, the men had gathered many passengers off-boarded from the nine hundred and seventy passengers packed on the train that had been altered on its course. Passengers were made to lie on the ground face-down, waiting for their fate.

One of the men came to Hamidu, where he lay, and in a voice hidden behind the scarf on the mouth he demanded for his phone. When he was unable to reach his trouser pocket, the man ransacked him quickly to obtain his phone. This had instilled more fear in other passengers around him because it was obvious to everyone that they were in a kidnapping situation, not necessarily a robbery. So soon, they were up on their feet, filed up and marched into the surrounding bushes.

Having walked for miles on their feet, the kidnapped passengers were walked deeper into bushes, culminating into a thick forest, just being led by the gun, herder's sticks and hands that slapped so hard when anyone slowed down the rest of the file. Two brave men made a run for it and were chased after and fired at until they were ensured dead. That was solely the unspoken warning they could give to all passengers to behave themselves, and it seemed everyone had caught the clear message.

A man, apparently the commander of the gang, asked them to stop and remove their shoes. From that point on, he told them they would be shoeless the entire journey because it would slow them down. The number of shoes collected and heaped to a side detailed more of the number of individuals there were in their captivity.

KEPRESSNG

A two-hour walk in the forest with thick tree canopies in layers, so far away from the explosion of the rail structure, would prevent aerial surveillance even if a search was conducted by the relevant authorities. The ongoing experience was so surreal for Hamidu. Few moments back, he was inside a cosy, air-conditioned coach of a train moving at twice the speed of a fast car, but now he was walking on his bare feet on a bush path with a painful bullet wound. He wondered how the fate of man could change in the twinkle of an eye.

"S-t-o-p!" the commander ordered again, and the tired body of the passenger responded. Many were sobbing quietly. Some were muttering something in faith to their God.

"Drop all your phones and other belongings, your wallet etc, in that bag over there. Empty all!" he said, pointing in the direction.

Everyone with gadgets on them moved in that direction. There were not many people since some people had lost their phones, handbags, and other belongings in the train explosion.

"Now, you will enter that ditch and take a dip," he decreed, pointing at it with a flashlight. "If I see your head up, I fire you."

The lead man of the gang had some of his men point flashlights into the ditch while each captive entered the large polythene-material-covered trench. The first on the line was a middle-aged woman who wanted to undress immediately but was stopped immediately.

"You go into it with your clothes," the lead man cautioned absolutely.

She entered it and screamed out loud. The rest of the captives online were taken over by fear, more fear. They could not tell whatever had happened to her inside it. Perhaps she was bitten by an animal right inside of it, but they also witnessed her come out of it wet. Thoughts of every one were wild at this point.

"I hear a sound from anyone, and your blood will fill the hole," the commander dished out words in anger again as he walked a distance away to smoke a cigarette.

"Thank me later when you are free of infection and night insect bites," he said in Fulani language, not caring if they understood it or not.

It soon came to Hamidu's turn. He moved down the dug entrance channelled into the ditch with polythene cover to prevent the fluid form from flowing out or seeping into the earth. He wondered how long the planning had taken to capacitate the thought of digging a full-size ditch as this, in the middle of a forest. He moved closer for a dip, and he could discern the smell of bleach from the poignant tang of the small pool. He also could smell so mildly antiseptic in the pool of solution. As he lowered himself, taking a dip, he could feel some hurtful sensations in the different parts of his body right from his feet, which had become sore from trekking. That suggested to him that it was not only a gunshot wound. He had some bruises and abrasions, too. On getting a full dip, the pain on his arm became agonizingly accentuated, and he also would have screamed to ease or relieve the hurt but grunted in deep pain as he bore the soreness in courage, coming out, one step after another. His body trembled from the ache as the night faded in his vision. He groggily walked out of it, and suddenly, he fell to the ground and almost passed out.

KEPRESSNG

One of the abductors ran to him, trying to see if he was still alive. Hamidu's eyes blinked from hurt as the man wiped them with his garment. He could barely see.

"Are you okay?" the man asked concernedly. "You would have to keep walking so you wouldn't be shot," he said, so low in a whisper.

Hamidu tried to open his eyes. There was some familiarity in the voice. He barely had his eyes open, and his vision was so blurry that he could only see an outlined image.

"I'm going to help you up your feet, and you will walk away now, please," the same voice persuaded.

He was helped to his feet and took wobbly steps one after the other to where others were calmly seated. He felt like he was losing it. Perhaps he was going to faint.

"We shall stay here briefly and leave by sunrise," the harsh voice of the commander quaked the attention of the abductees once again. "And if I hear any sound of movement from anyone, anywhere, I will make meat of you."

The night was cold. Having wet clothes on did not help the chills. Hamidu felt sick; his mouth was very dry. He had contemplated drinking from the ditch earlier on, but it was too caustic to taste, and his dehydrated body needed water desperately. The abductees lay in rows of fifteen by ten men apart in a clearing. They were separated from the females, who were a smaller group in a different place not entirely far from the men, so close eyes could be on them all. Nevertheless, they had their own guards, just like the men.

One of the guards with an AK 47 assault rifle hanging on his neck moved in line, close to where Hamidu lay on his side of the arm was uninjured. His breathing was rapid and heavy. His body was getting cold, and he was beside himself. The guard stopped by Hamidu and asked if he was fine, but he could not get an answer from him because Hamidu was shivering from the cold of the night.

"Never mind," a voice cautioned. It was the lead man. "I'll attend to him."

"Yes sir," the guard replied and moved away for the approaching lead man, who obviously had some respect accorded his command.

He bent over Hamidu to examine him.

"You have tried. You did well," the lead man praised. "I brought something to make you feel better." He tried to raise Hamidu's head to give him some liquid from the water bottle in his hands. Hamidu declined. He was reluctant. He thought he was about to be poisoned.

"I won't poison you brother," the lead man whispered slowly. "We are blood." he said, removing the scarf, preventing more than half of his face from being seen.

In the dull light of the half moon, Hamidu could see the figure looked like Salisu, though his imagery was blurry in his eyes.

"Salisu?"

"Shhhh!!!" he hushed him up with a finger placed across his lip. "I am Godogodo. Now drink, it is a herb to preserve your life," he concluded, pulling his head closer to his body.

"Didn't the commander say we should give neither water nor food to the captors?" the voice of the same guard nearby queried.

"I am, first of all, a human before a kidnapper," he snapped. "Now get out of here! Soulless being."

KEPRESSNG

Hamidu made an effort to seep from the bottle. It was bitter, but he was encouraged to take more of it for relief of his pain and recuperation. He soon fell into a deep slumber in the hand of one of his captors.

At the dawn of another day in captivity, Hamidu did not hear the wake-up call. The effect of the so-called herb was strong on him. It was soporific. The man who slept next to him had been trying to get him up, but he did not move until a guard came and kicked him hard with his boot. He rose with a shriek, his arm hurting from the booting that had it shifted from its laid position. He jumped up on his feet amidst the pain. The guard said nothing to him, but he could see his red eyes obviously glazed and titivated with the ardent power of marijuana. He probably needed not to say a word; his eyes did. Hamidu could recognize him from the night before. He hovered around them while they lay to sleep.

It was still dark, and one man amongst them hinted that it was just three o'clock in the morning from his broken watch. He said they must have had intel that the authorities were closing in on them, so they were moving the lot in such a short time. The abductors put them together in files of four rows so they could easily see the end of the line, the first man to the last man. Hamidu thought they were being treated like historical slaves when captured and filed up to the ship in chains. The only difference in their place was that there were no chains on them, but they were still captives not of their own free will anyway, he thought.

He suddenly remembered yesterday night. It had all happened so fast, and now his hands had been bandaged with white linen, though it still had some blood stains but seemed better and felt better. It was a saviour's mercy that he had. He looked out for him, but he was not in the crowd of people. They journeyed on their bare feet, with thick grasses and prickling stones under their feet, into the jungle, on paths known only to the abductors.

The paths got clearer to walk as the sky brightened for the day. It was obvious how white everyone looked on the skin from the solution of the night before. They would have walked for three to four hours into some part of the forest that seemed darkest, judging by the thickness of the canopy of trees. Tired from the long walk with sore feet, they thirsted for water, but no one dared to ask, though a stream was just about a hundred meters away.

"Anyone who wants to drink water is free," the commander said.

A number of people rushed forward, and the sound of a gun firing followed. This came from the gun of the commander putting a stop to every foot on the move; some fell on their knees, and others screamed out of fear.

"Did I give you permission to move together?" he asked, enraged in his voice. "Henceforth, anyone who disobeys orders shall be shot. You are too much already" He paused for a moment, his eyes scanning the length and breadth of the hoard of people.

"A-n-i-m-a-l-s!" he finally said and spat out contemptuously to his side.

The commander moved away, and five of his men came forward. They selected the first thirty people to drink water from the stream. Hamidu was one of the selected, but his reluctant feet, like many others, were almost unwilling to move again. Their thirst seemed to have dried up in the presence of fear and water. He, however, launched forward when pushed forward by the nozzle of the gun. A few others were treated alike, and that singular action quickened their confused steps towards the stream.

At the stream, they cupped their hands to bring water to their mouths. The action was repeated as much as the individual was satisfied. Some people choose to wash their faces and hands in the flowing water.

The lead man he had spotted yesterday suddenly appeared by his side, removed the scarf from his face, and started to drink water like others.

"Salisu?" Hamidu whispered in disbelief.

"No! Godogodo," he corrected. "Keep washing and drinking. No one must know we talk."

"Is this what you do?"

"I saved your life. I removed the bullet from your body. Thankfully, it didn't lodge in your bones."

"Is this what you do? Why are you doing this?" He washed his face pretentiously as he asked.

"I tried to live responsibly. After finishing school, I searched for legitimate jobs for a long time until someone introduced this job to me. I needed to survive."

"Kidnapping? A job?"

"Our society does not care how you make your money; just make money, and you'd be respected or even celebrated."

"That has not called for this."

"Our politicians, are they any better than I am? They have turned your life and my life into this mess. They have made everything impossible, and even feeding has become a problem of its own. We all strive to survive daily."

"You can justify yourself for all you want, Salisu," Hamidu said with exasperation, trying to get up, but he was pulled back in anger.

"They take our lives per second with their corruption, but nobody questions. I am a product of the corruption of our leaders. I am prepared to die for my transgressions even though I have not taken a life yet!" He affirmed with sternness, "Are they willing to do the same? Are they willing to die for their corruption? Many have died of their corruption than they have died in captivity."

The lead man rose up and looked around to ascertain any suspicious eyes around. Nobody seemed to pay attention, so he left the stream area and called the group back. Another thirty were next in line for water.

It was the sixth day, the rail structure that was rigged with an improvised explosive that had damaged the train AK-49 en route Kaduna State, resulting in hundreds of hostages being taken, some passengers missing while some were accounted dead. The government and the military forces were reportedly doing all they could to secure the release of hostages from the marauding bandits who had demanded ransom in hundreds of millions to secure the release of passengers, most of whom were first-time users of the newly commissioned train service.

Many of the hostages' immediate family members were contacted by the kidnappers for ransom to the tune of tens of millions of Naira for the release of their loved ones. Each victim's phone was used to contact their families. Hamidu and some others were set aside because they did not have phones they lay claims to. Each locked phone was asked to be unlocked by the user and thoroughly scrutinized for bank alerts and other monetary transactions. This was the foremost basis of best judgment for monetary demand from families of victims. Other ways of judgment were family names, physical looks of the hostage, professions, addresses, cost and quality of phones, and even mere instincts, amongst other sundry ways.

"Hey, you," the lead man pointed to Hamidu. "Come here"

Hamidu stepped forward, wondering what Salisu's plots were. He had been playing the game of pretence along with him since he revealed the man behind the scarf he was. He should appear an absolute stranger like every other.

"What's your name?"

"Hamidu."

"How is your hand? Hope it's healing?" he said, approaching Hamidu.

"It's getting better."

"I have an ointment for you to keep applying. It will help" He handed him a small plastic bottle. "Tell them you don't have a phone, no matter what happens. You are a student, no matter the shake-up," he whispered to him. There, it suddenly dawned on him that he was the one who searched and removed his phone from his pocket. So it was clearer to him that all along he had seen him in the crowd of passengers by the train.

He came close and whispered in his usual manner.

"You need not worry. You shall be saved sooner or later". He said and left his side.

Hamidu could not fathom his words. It did not carry the weight of hope, judging by what he and other people in captivity were going through and the time they had spent. It was merely six days, but it seemed like six months as each day dragged on and was full of untold hardship and torture. He had already started giving up on being free. Freedom was certainly going to be at a price, which, if not bought or taken advantage of, could be as costly as life.

It was the sixth day in captivity, where he had no access to medical care, and his legs were now swollen. He could barely walk without feeling pain. He was also aware that if he became a liability to his abductors by being incapacitated in whatever form, he would be wasted. People's lives meant nothing to many of the criminals with arms that he was sure.

The basics, such as feeding, were done once in two days and on a meagre ration that could only satisfy a little child. The meals were not palatable; captives only ate to satisfy hunger and stay alive. Weight loss was the first thing to be noticed in captives. The long-distance walk, dehydration, starvation and anxiety were the recipes for continuous weight loss. The captive situation was a situation in which the people had given up on hope because they were dehumanized and treated like inducement for money. Some people had been videoed beaten, in their agonizing state, asked to beg for help, pleading with friends and family to do something about their situation, portraying hostages as if they were condemned to death for no reason or fault of theirs.

Salisu rarely came around him anymore, surely for the best of reasons, but he could read pain in his eyes whenever he glanced at him. He was certainly unhappy, maybe for him, his state or the general condition of dehumanization of people. He has not lost the humanness in him.

It was time for another hostage profiling. The handpicked passengers were separated from the general lot. Hamidu had been grouped into this session. They were going to be asked questions under duress to extract information from them since they had no phone for primary scrutinization. He had witnessed from afar how some were treated in the process of trying to extract information from them. It was not a good sight for him, not at all.

He had been put as number two to start with. The number one captive had been dragged into the presence of the torturer, who happens to be the commander. He was threatened to be struck with a glinting machete, but each time the metal head landed on his body, it was the flat side. It was safe that he did not get a cut from it. However, it would have been terrorising and painfully agonising. For the rest of the captives that watched, it was death ahead of time.

Regretfully, Hamidu was not sure he could maintain the state of adamance Salisu had asked of him. Courage could break in the face of torment. There were no guarantees.

The man was crying uncontrollably like a baby when he was being drilled with questions. His answers to questions were spontaneous amidst loud snort-crying. He could see the commander dialling a number the man offered and was now conversing in his usual harsh tone. He heard him mention fifty million Naira as ransom for the man, or he would make sure he splatter his blood all over the camp. His gruelling voice resonated around. He had handed over his phone to the man who did his best to persuade his relatives to sell and garner as much. In about ten to fifteen minutes, the brutality was over, and the badly beaten captive was taken away.

Hamidu was next in line. He was helped up from the ground he sat on and led carefully to where he would be drilled with questions.

He sat face to face on a crudely constructed stool made of untreated forest wood, with the commander of the gang of kidnappers alone. It was as though he was given a seat with the Devil himself. His eyes were sunken and devoid of human empathy, and the practices of crime were evident in his look, voice, and entire being.

"Who are you?" he asked in an uncertain voice and tone.

"My name is Hamidu….. Hamidu Ibrahim," he stuttered.

"What do you do for a living?"

"I am a student," he lied. "I am about to be posted for my National Youth Service."

"Of what use is serving your motherland?" he queried in his customary now angry tone.

Suddenly, there were gunshots fired and repetitive returns of gunfire. A shout came from within the camp. Then, more gunfire and bullets were flying around. The commander hurriedly picked up his gun from a tree on one side and disappeared from Hamidu's presence in the direction away from the camp.

"You are surrounded," a voice from the megaphone said in Hausa.

Instinctively, Hamidu lay down flat on the ground, observing the chaos in the camp while playing safe on the ground. The captives, he observed, were lying down too. The only people on their heels were the evil men in the camp.

"Surrender Now!" the voice came on again.

Some of the kidnappers hid behind large Eucalyptus trees to gain sight and fire back randomly while they made their escape. Some more laid on the ground in military fashion to fight back until death, and few others laid down their weapons in surrender.

Consequently, at the end of the ten-minutes gun duel that seemed like forever evermore, the combating kidnappers were overpowered while some escaped into the larger forest, and a few surrendered to the soldiers who had occupied the camp.

The captives were liberated by the military. Every surviving captive was full of joy for the lease of hope of living. Many were full of thankful words to providence for his watchfulness and absolute care for them all through. Hamidu was asked to be placed on a stretcher after the headcount and preliminary examination of captives carried by the soldiers and medics. While he was being carried away on a stretcher to the waiting ambulance by two soldiers, Hamidu looked out for his brother, Salisu, but he did not see him. He observed that nine bodies were counted dead from the fierce battle. All bodies were that of neutralised woodland marauders; amongst them, which looked like Salisu from afar, was retrieved a signalling phone that had led the military authorities close to the environs of the nearest telecom cell site. They had accordingly tracked it down to the kidnappers' camp after a call was made to army headquarters by an unknown caller.

AYO-DANIEL O. AYODEJI, a versatile wordsmith born in Lagos, Nigeria, is a writer, playwright, and poet with a passion for storytelling deeply ingrained in his being. His literary journey began within the esteemed literary circles of the Association of Nigerian Authors, where his lifelong love for literature flourished.

Ayo-Daniel's literary repertoire spans various genres, from fantasy and contemporary fiction to literary fiction, plays, and poetry, captivating readers with his vivid imagination and masterful storytelling.

As an editor at Reporterscorp Newsly, he showcases his editorial acumen. Outside his professional life, Ayo-Daniel finds joy as a husband and father, drawing inspiration from his family as he continues to craft tales that resonate globally..

THE VISIT

– Buluma Bwire

"No honey, today's not a day for orange, purple, or red on those luscious black lips."

"Go subtle, try nude."

"Subtle?"

"Subtle, how now? I thought the theme was 'loud and bold'."

"Um, yeah. But more bold and less loud, I think."

"How's that even possible, babe?"

"Not sure, honey, but we have to make it subtle."

So, here I stand, giving fashion pointers on shades of everything from clothes to lipstick. My forte, usually. But, today is unusual. A normal visit has taken on the gravitas of a state visit and blinded my eye for fashion. In its place are dark, muted, and neutral hues of self-doubt that I struggle to saturate into brightness. Brightness of thought. Yet, in defiance of all my efforts, the ever-growing mound of discarded clothing that arranges itself around my feet betrays the lie that I know what I am doing. Everything is a measure short. Too short. Too revealing. Too snug. Too skimpy. Too concealing. Too much. Too little.

The inadequacies of my wardrobe choices compete with my own feelings of inadequacy at this impending visit, itself clothed as a function. Or is it a celebration masquerading as a function and presenting as a visit? I didn't know. I don't know. I don't want to know.

Too many thoughts present too many choices but not enough subtle options. Incensed, I head to the living room to ask for a third opinion from our reliable third-wheeler, Clyde.

"Well, what do you think?"
"About what?"
"About us?"
"Who is us?"
"Us!"
"Honey! Get yourself out here! It's Clyde for the tiebreaker!"

I indulge in my favourite stress reliever, shouting. Bellowing a commanding falsetto to summon my beau into the living room from the bathroom where she has taken up temporary residency.

"Hmmm. Now, didn't you say she's hardcore conservative?" The question is about my mother-in-law-to-be, the sole beneficiary of my myriad wardrobe changes. Today is 'parents' day for my beau and me. Or is it the first day of the rest of our lives? Ironically, it is not my maiden visit, but every time, it seems like the first time and not like the last time. However, this time is the first time of a new time and the last time of an old time. Or is it simply time?

Instead of the hyped rainbows and butterflies, my thoughts are blackened with dark thoughts and Purple

Emperors. Purple Emperors. Butterflies still. Beautiful even. Resplendent in their indigo blue and white speckled wings underlain by a coal-black layer. But they feed on rotting flesh and faeces while deliberately avoiding flowers. These are the thoughts that assail my mind as I consider the intricate relations that constitute the institution of marriage and its custodians - family, society, religion, state.

"This is it!"

Clyde's voice knifes its way through my thoughts with his verdict.

"You! Keep the top and go get the brown skirt that you had on two outfits ago."

"And you! That blue woven chiffon saree with the paige blouse will have you steal all eyes in the room. Keep it."

"This is it!" he yells with conclusiveness.

The jury is out, and the verdict is in favour of the brown ensemble. Subtle.

I rush back into the bedroom to put on the almond-coloured knee-length skirt, snuggle up in the beige silk blouse, and taper down to the nude high heels. All was complemented facially with just a trace of brown lipstick. There was no blush today, but maybe just a touch of eyeshadow- brown. For jewellery, I shall stick with my rose gold wristwatch.

I meet my beau in the living room, resplendent in her saree and flats. Our choice of wardrobe is a Freudian projection of our upbringing. Therein comes the barrier wielded by the custodians of the institution of marriage - family, society, religion, state. But we are fighting back tooth and nail. 'Love Will Conquer All', Lionel Richie's soothing voice is our battle cry. We cry our eyes dry every time we hit the lines of the fourth verse,

'... *Why is the world so unkind... can't we see that* .'

"Beep!!"

That's Clyde furiously tooting the car horn, a signal for us to come out. I don't blame him. We are notorious for our wardrobe changes. Then again, we are renowned for our wardrobe tastes. Exotic tastes, like real emperors. Purple Emperors. It evens out.

"We are coming!" we yell out in practised mischief.

"Yes, you both like coming. A lot. That's the problem!" An inside joke.

With that, we dash out and hop into the love of Clyde's life. A seventh generation BMW 3 series presenting as the G20 saloon with a six-cylinder engine and semi-autonomous drive alongside adaptive voice and gesture control. This is the wagon with which we ride into the sun-drenched horizon of another day in this never-ending love story starring my beau and me.

The low burble of the BMW six-cylinder engine contrasts with the distant murmur of thoughts assailing my mind. Questions, mostly. Questions without answers. Why is it that we attach so much importance to other people's opinions concerning any and every aspect of our lives? Validation of a society that itself craves validation for the myriad prejudices it has constructed as its guiding morals? Morals that have been distilled into instruments of hate dispensed by adherents of otherwise all-loving deities of all shades of mankind? Adherence that has resulted in the legislation of these morals and the persecution of those who fall outside this moral landscape?

Questions. Questions. Questions. All I have are questions, no answers. These questions are foremost in my mind as I settle myself into the back seat of the car. A prelude to the psychological preparation for today's encounter with my prospective mother-in-law.

"Why are you in such a pensive mood?" my beau asks when she notices my trance-like state as her hands snaked their way into mine.

Then her luscious lips parted to reveal a set of perfectly cut teeth, white as pearls encased in a light brown oyster. Slowly, she breaks into that bewitching grin that I fell in love with the first time it was directed my way to light up my whole being. When it's coupled with a stare from those lovely brown eyes, eyes so intent I continually drown in them, my heart melts, and my legs turn into jelly from the thighs down. That's not all, for my breath comes in short gasps of air, and I lose my faculty of speech - to say nothing about thought. To crown it all, my heart beats with the ferocity of a caged lion seeking release. And when she touches me…it's all over. Release! I don't care what anybody says, thinks, or does. She is mine. And I am not losing her for anything or anybody. EVER.

My beau's smile works its magic; it calms me. Speaking without words that's our thing. But this time, I give voice to the darkening clouds in my head.

"Oh, honey, if only your mother could love us for us. Not for others."

"Babe, relax. We talked, she listened, and she accepted. Us for us."

"I know. But. It was just us then, now, there are others."

"It does not matter. It has always been mom and me. Us against the world. Others, well, they are just others. And when it mattered most, they 'othered' mom and me - then it was just us. So, it's just us, but now three instead of two."

My beau is an eternal optimist, with nothing but rainbows and butterflies in her world view.

No Purple Emperors.

"Traaafiiiik is busy but movin."

A rainbow cocktail of accents. European? British? American? Everything in-between? That's the radio presenter nasally penetrating our conversation; Clyde's turned up the volume. His way of switching the conversation to more neutral ground.

"Eish! Why does this African speak through the nose?" Clyde is onto his favourite rant.

"Well, darling, you need to get that deep African baritone on air asap!" I chided him.

"Give me a mic and a studio. I'd do it now now."

"Yoh! Stop. You just passed mom's gate," my beau calls our attention back to the road. One U-turn later, we are at the French wrought iron gates that announce the opulence of the homestead beyond.

"Hello, guests have already arrived. Waiting, all waiting, waiting for you." The gate guard mouths these words to greet us as he comes to open the gate.

I can't help wondering why? Why are they waiting? For us?

Dark clouds. Purple Emperors.

"What, no jokes today?" my beau asks the gate guard.

He usually stages an elaborate performance of scanning the car and its occupants before cracking a joke or two about empty stomachs and dry throats. A cue for some change to be pressed into his palm. An African tradition. Subtle extortion. But this time, he just grins and mock salutes while waving us through.

Maybe he has collected enough gate tax?

Maybe he is high on traditional beer?

Maybe there is no reason?

Maybe I just let it be?

We pass through a tree colonnade that is a fastidious arrangement of greenery and wind our way down to the veranda of the main house. My beau's mother is already opening the door.

"Hugs, Kisses!"

"Kisses, Hugs!"

Secret greetings between a mother and her child, excluding the rest of the world in their intimacy.

"Hello, my children." That's for the rest of us. Clyde and me.

We step into the house and make our way to the lounge, where the seated mass of strangers rises to meet us. Greet us. Hugs, partially. Handshakes, mostly. Mostly handshakes and conscious stares, no kisses.

I meet the conscious stares with gazes into their eyes. I see black and brown pupils dancing in cloud white seas, with a touch of blood red for those who were early on the liquor trail. That is all I see with my naked eye. But in my mind's eye, they all merge and *metamorph* into blazing coals of hellishly fierce intensity. These visions from my mind's eye have me instantly lowering my gaze. A flash mob about to descend on a royal flush of Purple Emperors.

I raise my gaze to find my beau's mother smiling. Hold that picture. She is smiling, and, oh my God, she is smiling at me!

Before you write me off as a card-carrying member of the lunatic club, allow me to bring you up to speed. I've been going out with my beau for nearly four years, during which time I discovered a rare phenomenon, a ninth worldly wonder. My beau's mother was smiling at me. The battle for her acceptance began in the third month of the first of these past four years.

Acceptance.

Acceptance of her, of me, of us.

Also, by her, by me, by us.

Acceptance of us for us.

I smile back. "Nice day for a barbecue, isn't it? Mom."

"Indeed, it is my child, indeed it is."

My hand instinctively straightens out my hair, blouse, and skirt. All at once. Signs of nervousness and the pressure to impress.

Got to have my best foot forward.

Iridescent. Regal. A Purple Emperor.

Must come out a winner now that I am out.

"Ladies, why don't we sit out on the back veranda?"

A loud, motherly voice booms through the lounge. I locate its origin in a well-fed and well-appointed mother figure, bedecked in pearls and wrapped in a flowery white pleated silk dress.

"Sure, why not? We really ought to spend some time away from all this testosterone."

Gender assignment through acclamation. Acclamation in the form of roaring male laughter. Not too sure where that leaves us 'visitors', though. Not too sure where to go. Very sure not to mingle with strangers, though. I unconsciously move towards Clyde and my beau. My safe space.

Our eyes meet across the crowded room, blind to the exchange of knowing smiles as we make our way towards each other, drawn together by a connection that is simply electric in its intensity. Nothing else matters. Nothing else exists. For that brief minute in time, we are the only ones in existence.

KEPRESSNG

Have you ever been in love?

The love that reignites itself into a searing flame every time you capture and hold your beau's gaze? You are instantly smouldering in the adoring gaze of those lovely eyes that are adoringly directed your way. You feel your heart melt, you go weak at the knees, and you lose your power of speech. Instead, all you can manage between the two of you is a series of coquettish giggles and monosyllabic sentences.

The sun seems to shine just a little bit brighter, the melody of the birds singing outside just a little bit sweeter, the air just a little bit fresher, and the atmosphere around the two of you is simply euphoric. All is right with the world, and you have never been happier... you are falling in love all over again, just like the first time you met, and each time is the first time.

"My child, what are you standing there like an extra leg for? Or have you become too much of a westerner to help your mother serve her guests?"

My beau meekly proceeds towards the sound of mom in the kitchen, her meekness belies the fact that I shall use such scenes to chide her for leaving me at sea. I can't follow. Guests don't go to people's kitchens uninvited.

"When in doubt, eat!" Clyde says and makes a beeline for the dining table, which is groaning under a bulk of delicacies. I follow in his wake.

"Here, come sit next to me." He taps a chair next to his. I oblige.

"Well, you seem ok."

"Why wouldn't I be?"

"Aren't you tense? Worried even?"

"About what?"

"About us? About here? About us being here?"

"Nope. I know what you are thinking. But three things. Money. Class. Exposure."

"What do you mean?"

"Exactly that. Money. Class. Exposure. All folks here have all three, and most live abroad. There is nothing here they haven't seen before."

"Ah, ok. I think."

Clyde loudly offers to pray for the bounty spread out before us, and I must exert maximum effort to avoid laughing out loud. I can never get him to say more than an 'Amen' in terms of prayer. He, however, manages to acquit himself honourably in that task. We serve. We eat. We chat. A brief respite from dark clouds and Purple Emperors.

Food, music, conversations. My ears prick up trying to pick up threads and wove them into a story I can pick up and contribute to, an invitation to mingle. No such luck. So, I take solemn comfort in the fact that I have Clyde by my side.

"Come on, let's make ourselves known and our presence felt."

"To whom, Clyde?"

"To your future in-laws, that's whom," Clyde says this with a finality that has the ring of a conclusion and promptly snakes his way through the room, a handshake here, a smile there, followed by a delicate introduction of us. I am more than happy to follow in the wake of this social butterfly.

"Are people chanting outside?" I ask after my ears pick up on a hypnotic rhythmic reiteration of words.

"Chanting or chatting?" asks Clyde.

"Shhhh! Listen…" But my attempts to filter out other sounds to tune in to the chant are suddenly stilled as a loud scream pierces the air.

KEPRESSNG

"BABE!!!"

My heart beats. My heart stops. My heart runs. My heart bleeds. I am a chaos of emotions, for I know that voice, the voice of my heart, the voice of the one I love. My mind races to process what's going on as my feet race towards the heart-rendering call, the intended recipient of which can only be me. It must be me. It is me.

But I never make it. My entire body is paralyzed, shocked to its core in an instant and then besieged with a searing, blinding pain. I am now a ball of pain, doubled over. I don't know what is happening. I can't think, and my brain's attempt to process is blinded by pain before it can catch up with the swift motion of my body towards the sound. I regress into animalistic functionality. I grunt, I howl, I scream, I sweat. But mostly, I just feel pain. Pain and more pain emanating from the back of my head at first. Then, it works its way down my spine and permeates the core of my being in rapidly incremental bursts.

I am being attacked!

Through the fog in my brain, the wheels slowly grind, and the penny drops.

I am being attacked!

I am being beaten!

I am being mobbed!

I am being killed?

But it is not about me. It was never about me. It has never been about me. It has always been about us. Us for us. I must get to my beau. I must save my beau. I must save us.

"Honey, hang on! I am coming!"

The command issued from my mind to my vocal cords is to scream and shout, and I croak. A primeval guttural sound.

"Cl-l-l-y-y-y-y-d-e?" not even a croak, now just a feeble whisper.

"Don't worry, my son."

Why is someone calling me their son? I am no one's son.

"Don't worry, boys. Prayers. Nothing but Prayers."

Boys? Prayers? I don't understand. I want this nightmare to end. Yes, that's what it must be: a nightmare. In a few seconds, I shall wake up safe in the hands of my beau.

But that does not happen.

More pain. Through rapidly swelling eyes, I spy Clyde on the floor. Bleeding. Why?

More pain. I am now outside. How did I get here?

More pain. Why is my blouse torn? Where are my shoes?

More pain. Where is my beau?

I see her blurred. Is it her? Can I see? Why can't I see?

"B-----aaa----bbb---ee"

More pain. It is her. I think. She screams. I hear her. It is her.

More pain. More people chanting and shouting about sons, boys, and prayers. And demons.

More pain. The pain of comprehension. The pain of betrayal. The pain of anguish. The pain of death. The pain of pain.

Baited. Wings shredded. The Emperor is dead! Long live the Emperor!

BULUMA BWIRE is invariably 'othered' by others because of a myriad of idiosyncrasies. He spends the better part of his existence chasing the threads of various stories that unravel in his head. Distillation of these stories to be imbibed by others is his life's passion, and hopefully will form the core of his life's work. Meanwhile, as he awaits the gods to smile upon the ink in his pens to give him sustenance, he moonlights as a lawyer and part-time academic.

MALI

— Ifeanyi Ogbo

Many decades before my father, Chukwukadibia, embarked on his journey to the afterlife, he undertook a monumental voyage from his hometown in Mbour, Senegal, to Enugu in Nigeria. There, he joined the workforce at the Ogbete mine. My father intended it to be a two-month assignment but spent the rest of his life in Enugu. Throughout his life, during innumerable dinners marked by copious amounts of pepper soup, palm wine, and conversations punctuated by the melodious clinking of cups and plates, my father would joke that my mother's beauty and kindness were the main reasons his two-month visit to Enugu turned into a lifetime commitment.

"That's the power of a beautiful, gracious, and brilliant woman. She came into my life, and I knew that going back to Senegal was not an option," he'd proclaim with a twinkle in his eye. My mother, ever the pragmatic one, would retort while laughing, "Don't listen to him; his quest for wealth is what kept him here."

To which my father, his gaze playfully directed at wherever my mother was seated, would counter, "And who am I spending all the money I made on?"

This exchange was a timeless dinner ritual. It always elicited hearty laughter, no matter how often it unfolded.

My father, whose birth name was Malik, adopted Chukwukadibia after settling in Enugu. His name was not the only thing he changed. Over the years, he wore many different hats in his career. He worked as a miner and sold precious stones. He also taught English and French, farmed, traded palm wine to the neighbouring villages, painted, and served as a clerk at the British office in town. He learned to speak Igbo like a local and became a beloved, contributing member of our village through his involvement in the Anglican church and various community initiatives.

Perhaps his most memorable role was at home. He was a loving husband to my mother, Akudo, and a caring father to my siblings, Nkemjika, Obiora, and me, Chikasi. He was also our friend, teacher, and jester who lured hidden laughter out of our souls.

He had an easy way of connecting with people, and on the day of his burial, the church could not hold back the mourners. They milled around the freshly dug earth, screaming at the top of their lungs.

"I've never told anyone this before. But, did you know your father paid my second son's school fees for three years after my husband died?" Akwaeke, a woman who sold children's clothes in the local market, whispered to me. "He swore me to secrecy not to tell anyone."

"Your father was very proud of you and your siblings. I always found it fascinating that whenever he came to offer his prayer requests and thanksgiving, it was always about his children," Sister Flora, one of the sisters of the praying band, confided in me.

Chief Nwosu, one of the oldest clansmen in the village, addressed my mother and I at the front of our home. "Our people say a digger of wells never runs out of water. Chukwukadibia had been in our village for six days when my barn caught on fire. The next couple of days, even though he didn't speak our language at the time or know me, he joined the youths to work. He helped in rebuilding my barn. He didn't have to perform any rituals to become a part of us. His kindness was more than a thousand rituals."

I was pulled to every corner and told of the goodness of my father. I appreciated all the kind words. But as the day went on and the burial process evolved into a feast and celebration of life as customs intended, I wanted to find a quiet place to sit and feast on my sadness.

The day before he died, I stopped by the house to drop some maize and vegetables for my parents. It had been a long day of teaching from dawn to dusk as the school exams were fast approaching. The Francis Memorial School, Ogbete, where I taught English literature and French, had admitted a record number of students in the past few months through a sensitization program organized by the government of the Eastern Region of Nigeria. This led to overcrowded classrooms.

By the end of most days, my voice was hoarse and my feet heavy. After classes ended at 4 pm, I went to my farm with two of my students, Mabel and Ekeama. We harvested maize cobs, pumpkin leaves, and tomatoes. Then, I cycled uphill with the goods to my parents. By the time I arrived, the sun had already set. The atmosphere was alive with the evening sounds of our village: pestles hitting against mortars in preparation for evening meals, children playing under the soft gaze of the moon, bicycles winding through open paths, crickets singing their song, and goats bleating theirs too.

My mother was in the kitchen, and I dropped the maize and vegetables on the brown table by the window. I could hear my father's voice streaming in from the living room, where he was doing baby talk with one-year-old Uchenna, Obiora's first child. I debated going in to say hello. But, I was bone-tired. I told myself I'd be back tomorrow, a Saturday, to spend more time with him. That did not happen, as he died in his sleep that night.

There are two layers to mourning: We mourn what we had and what could have been but never will. I found myself submerged between both layers. My father had been present for most of my life's highlights, and the fact that he would not be there for the ones to come crushed me. There were days I felt like I was dreaming and begged my chi to wake me up. When it became clear that he was dead, I prayed to see him in my dreams. I prayed for him to visit me. And, for us to have one more conversation over a walk like we always did.

For many weeks, nothing happened; his burial came and went, but there was no message from him. I had dreamless nights and nights when my exhausted mind replayed the events of the day. Then, one night, three months after he had passed on, I had a dream.

It was late September, the final days of the rainy season. I had been reading a book by the window until my candle melted away. Lying on my mat, I drifted into slumber while praying with my rosary. In the dream, I found myself wearing a purple and white gown. It was an adult version of my favourite childhood dress. I strolled across a vast expanse of golden sand. The sun warmed me, the wind ruffled my afro, and a soft, melodious hum surrounded me. It was as if nature was singing a silent song.

I had no specific destination in mind, and I wasn't troubled by it. Each step I took felt like a prayer; every breath I drew was a psalm. I had walked quite a distance when someone appeared by my right side. It was my father. At first, we exchanged no words but shared happy smiles and walked together, much like two children who had reconnected after a long separation and had no need for words to express their joy. My father had on a large yellow boubou, and his head and fingers were adorned with gold. After a while, he stopped and pointed to the sun.

"The sun is setting, Nwa'm. I must head back."

I gazed up, and indeed, the sun was making its descent.

"Please, don't go, Papa."

"I'm going back to where I came from, but I'll always be with you," he reassured.

He began to retreat. As he did, everything around us lost its colour and faded into darkness with each passing second. Tears welled up in my eyes as I asked:

"How do I find you again, Papa?"

He paused, then replied, "Go to a town called Iduren. I'll be reincarnated there, and they will name me Mali."

"Please don't leave me, Papa," I pleaded, weeping as the world dissolved into pitch black.

KEPRESSNG

"Do not worry, my child. I'm never far from you. Go out into the world and never forget all that I've taught you. You are light, You are the earth's delight, and the bird of grace forever nests atop your heart. Go share that grace" His voice faded into the distance.

Overhead, the moon appeared, and I heard the soothing sound of waves from an ocean I hadn't noticed earlier. By the shores of this unfamiliar sea, I knelt and wept. I awoke with tears still in my eyes and heard the sky crying through a heavy thunderstorm that persisted throughout the night.

I jotted down the words 'Iduren' and 'Mali' in my notebook, clinging to the memory of the encounter with my father in the dream. By the faint light of a lamp, I looked up Iduren in the encyclopaedia of Nigeria I had in my little library. I had goosebumps when I discovered it was a small town on a hill in the middle belt of the country.

I had to go visit. This was perfect timing as the school was on a holiday break, and I had free time. I stayed up till dawn, drawing up a plan for my visit. By the time the first cock crowed, I had a plan and felt a surge of joy I had not felt in a long time. I had to tell my mother and brother about my dream and plan. Cleaning off the raindrops from my bicycle, I balanced the encyclopaedia and a small basket of Okpa in the front and set out to my destination.

I pedalled full throttle on my bicycle, rolling through the lush farms that bordered the winding pathway leading to my mother's home. My hands danced in the air, a hazy greeting to the blurred faces of people by the roadside, their greetings lost amidst the windswept rush. In the distance, the ethereal voices of altar boys serenaded the morning with 'Adoramus te Christe,' a

Latin hymn that mingled in sync with the wind's gentle whoosh and the chorus of awakening birds. It was a blend of sounds never to be woven together quite the same way again in my lifetime. At that moment, my soul ached to shout my joy to the world, to proclaim that my dream of having a dream had finally come true.

My mother was in the living room when I arrived. She mentioned that Obiora, my brother, had stepped out to get some firewood. We ate the Okpa and talked about last night's rain as we waited for Obiora's return. When he came back an hour later, I told them about the dream and my intention to travel to find the baby my father had reincarnated into. There was silence for a few minutes after I finished, and then Obiora spoke up.

"Why will Papa decide to reincarnate in a distant town? My wife is pregnant with our second child. He needs to come back through the child, and if it's a boy, I will name him Nnamdi to honour his rebirth. Being reborn in a town none of us had heard of till now makes no sense." He turned to look at Mother as if to nudge her to affirm his words. But she sat silently with her head bowed.

When she finally spoke, her voice was shaky, "I am not surprised your father revealed that to you. He loved varying cultures and people. You know he came from Senegal and travelled to many other countries before he settled here. Even when he stopped travelling, he kept reading, which is a form of travel in its own way. Remember how he'd discover fascinating stories about foreign cultures and tell us about them in dramatic form over dinner?"

I chuckled at the recollection of my father's exaggerated rendition of cultural stories. I hoped in this new incarnation, he'd be an actor or a writer. Two things he didn't explore in the lifetime we had with us.

"I'm glad he is back," Mother continued, "your father always wanted to explore the whole of Nigeria, but he only visited the west and the east, so it makes sense he came back to a place he did not visit before he passed on. I think your brother should accompany you on this trip. Nkemjika would have joined if she had come back from Onitsha. Either way, you both have my blessings."

The next couple of days were a flurry of activities. We bought herbs and soup ingredients for the mother, coconut oil, wrappers, powder, and an assortment of dried fruits. Mother sewed some baby clothes. A week was delegated for the entirety of the trip. That would give us enough time to forestall the difficulty of finding a mother and child and enough time to be with them. Hours before the trip, in the deep throes of the night, Obiora's wife Paulina gave birth to twin girls, and we decided at dawn for me to set out alone.

I got into a rickety taxi that would take me to Udi, from where I'd find a bus heading out to towns in the middle belt, Iduren inclusive. As we drove through a road flanked by Araba trees, I saw Ugo, the town drunk, standing by the crumbling uno aja, the village's watchtower. He looked sober for the first time in a long time, and when the bus made a turn through where he stood, he stretched out his hand into the taxi and gave me a bundle of leaves. It was an array of different plant stalks all taped together to a thick stem. I tossed the strange gift away when I got to Udi, but days later, I'd remember the gift and marvel at its significance in the journey that unfolded.

The bus drive to Iduren was filled with a colourful cast of characters. There was an Atilogwu dance troupe going to perform in Lokoja for the Independence celebration. They were dressed in their full regalia – a heady mix of vivid yellow, red, and orange hues. Their dancing ankle tambourines filled the air with music with every move they made. People once believed that Atilogwu dancers were involved in black magic.

My father once told me he found it fascinating that, at the sight and sound of people doing beautiful things with their bodies, the first thing some people did was blame it on sorcery. They didn't see the tremendous power of the body and soul connecting. There were three men with six caged hyenas. They used the hyenas for performances across the country. There were also a couple of farmers and a plump woman who was a herbalist. She was selling an herbal drink she claimed would make you add weight in two days. It was with this eclectic mix that the bus drove northward through towns enveloped with endless dust, stalls selling blood-red tomatoes and peppers, flag rag ferryboats, loud spice markets, children excited by the sight of a bus, and beaten paths created by cows and sheep.

Throughout the trip, people alighted at their destinations until I was the last person left on the bus with the driver. We arrived at the town by 6.30 pm. At the entrance of the town was a signboard that said, "Welcome to Iduren, where there are no strangers, only long-lost family." There were donkeys with carriages behind them. I explained to Yousouf, one of the riders, that I was going to the hospital and boarded one. The atmosphere in Iduren was filled with a sense of calmness that made me feel relaxed and rejuvenated despite the long trip I had just taken. Perhaps it was the abundance of trees, the rolling hills, the fresh air, the leisurely pace of the town, or a combination of all that made me feel this way.

We drove past an evening market where laughing men in long kaftans sold jugs of Arabian tea and women in colourful gowns sold fruit. They had the biggest watermelons and pineapples I'd ever seen. We went past quiet farms, small houses, and a large open field where dozens gathered in prayer under the wide dome of the sunset sky.

We rode at a steady pace till we got to a one-storey building painted cornflower blue, which Yousouf said was the maternity home. I alighted, grabbed my bags, and headed to the reception area, where I requested to have an audience with the head midwife.

After waiting for fifteen minutes, I was directed to a room further down the building, and as I walked past the room, I could hear babies crying. It made my heart skip a beat to think that my reincarnated father could be one of the babies. The label on the door of the room read 'Head Midwife: Nurse Nahum.' I knocked, and a tall, stately woman with a wild cloud of grey hair opened the door.

She peeked at me with soft brown eyes over the rims of her large horned glasses and gestured me in. "Welcome," she said. "I heard you've come from a town far away to see a baby, but first, you must join me to have some hibiscus tea. I have it every evening in between my work rounds. It's freshly brewed from the hibiscus plant that is grown in the mission garden and so good for the spirit and body."

She poured out a cup of hibiscus tea from a jug for me, and I drank it. Taking in the tartness of the tea, the whiffs of cinnamon and ginger, and slight hints of honey. I felt so deeply at peace that I almost cried from the relief I felt.

"I'm looking for a baby named Mali," I said, slowly keeping down the cup of tea.

"What do you mean?"

For the first time since I had the dream, I shared it with a stranger without leaving out any details.

When I was done, Nurse Nahum sat looking at me, her mouth agape and far from the sense of composure she had when I first walked in.

"Are you very sure your father said Mali from the town of Iduren?"

"Yes, he did."

She took off her glasses. "I think your father was trying to tell you he is still with you through everyone you see around you. Over here in Iduren, "Mali" means human. Some also use it to refer to every living being. That's not all. Everyone here bears the name Mali. Every single person. My full name is Nurse Nahum Abba Mali."

She paused to take a sip of her tea and continued, "There are two stories about the origin of the name. I'll share them with you. The first is about an old man named Kale. Centuries ago, he found himself in the sober presence of grief, mourning the departure of his beloved wife, Mali. With a heart torn yet hopeful, he prayed for a reunion, yearning for one last shared moment over a comforting cup of tea reminiscent of times long gone.

In his dreams, a message reached Kale from the spirits of his ancestor, assuring him that his earnest plea had been heard. Mali would grace him with her presence in three days, and he was tasked with the tender preparation of a tea brewed from chosen leaves from the garden, ripe lemons, sun-dried dates, clove oil, and wild honey. Additionally, he was to prepare brown rice cakes, a delicacy that held a special place in Mali's heart.

As the anticipated day unfolded, Kale brewed a fresh jug of tea, blending flavours he knew Mali would love. The house came alive with the inviting aroma of tea and the familiar warmth of brown-rice cakes, patiently waiting for Mali's return.

Kale sat by the table with the tea in anticipation. Hours later, there was a knock and a little girl with a dog stood by the door and requested a cup of tea and some cake, for she was famished from playing in the fields. He told her he wished he could help, but he was saving the tea and cake he had for Mali and couldn't give her any of it at this point.

Hours passed, and another knock echoed through Kale's abode. This time, a pregnant woman and a man with a camel sought some food for their journey to a distant town. With regret, Kale shared his predicament, expressing his inability to part with the awaited tea and cakes.

Hours after they left, just as the sun was setting, there was yet another knock. It was a group of men from a distant town who were passing by on their way to a neighbouring town to go dig wells for the king there. They told him they were hungry and needed some tea and cakes, and he relayed the same story he had told the previous visitors.

Night enveloped the world, and wearied by the passing hours, Kale dozed off in a rocking chair, still awaiting Mali's arrival. In his dreams, his ancestor appeared once more. Kale, disheartened by Mali's absence, expressed his lament. With a gentle rebuke, the ancestor spoke:

"Bless your simple heart. She, in her excitement, came for tea with you in multiple forms, yet each time, you turned her away."

We both sat in silence, contemplating the first story; then she continued with the second one.

"There is a river that separates this town from the neighbouring town of Bassu, and centuries ago, some unresolved issues between both towns led to a war. After the elders of both lands reached a truce and ended the war, they decided to use this joint name as a unifying factor to remind us that even if a river separates us, our souls are all connected. This heritage has been passed on from generation to generation; every baby born in this town has Mali added to their name. Of course, this does not solve every problem, but it's a beautiful, ever-present reminder of our shared humanity.

You are Mali, and so am I.

All divisions between anything in our cosmos are despotic. The cosmos is a single, enormous entity. Any division we humans create is like splitting a river into two sides, with one side designated River One and the other River Two. Although it can help differentiate objects, it is ultimately unreal. We are all one entity."

I nodded my head at her words. Despite exiting this plane, Father was still teaching us lessons. He was opening our eyes to see the world in a different way. If I prepared his favourite meal and shared it with someone who had no food, I was feeding him. If I ever missed him and hugged my sister, I was hugging him.

The sound of babies crying from one of the rooms filtered in. I put the gifts I brought gently on the table.

"These are gifts for Mali from my family," I explained, sharing a smile with Nurse Nahum.

"Here's to Mali," she responded, raising her tea.

"To Mali," I replied, raising mine in agreement.

I thought my father would come back as a little boy with the legs of a gazelle or a little girl with eyes the colour of honey. But, he had come back as every human. He was here as every human who once existed, who still exists, and who will exist someday. An ever-spiralling branch in the eternal tree of the universe.

IFEANYI OGBO is an accomplished author of two poetry collections, A Forever Kind of Dream and Alive In The Memory Of Stars and a short story collection, A Backpack Filled With Sunsets.

In addition to his literary pursuits, he finds pleasure in activities such as reading, hiking, and traveling.

He lives in Nigeria

TUG OF DEFIANCE

— *Ikechukwu Henry*

The hall was boxed in a cauldron of silence, so deep, swallowing all sounds and leaving nothing but stillness in its wake, and Emeka began to wonder if everyone had become mute. Then, murmuring exploded like the hum of a bee, and applause echoed through the hall like a symphony.

Emeka felt proud of himself and of the speech he delivered, one that would linger in the minds of his captivated audience for a while. He strutted down the podium with an egoistic gait; his demeanour seemed to be remiss of the smile sprawling over the faces of his audience. Emeka hopped down from the podium, handshaking people, suddenly clustered around him as he made his way out of the hall.

"Your speech was a tapestry of thought, provoking and introspective!" remarked a young man with a lofty appearance - hunched shoulders, calloused hands, arms rippled with muscles. Emeka thought his fingers would snap when the young man's hand curled around his. He smiled at the squeeze, muttering 'thank you' in a low hum, and he was sure the young man must be a law student either in his final year or still starting out.

"Prof, I love your speech. It highlights our inner thoughts," a lecturer, whose face flashed with familiarity yet eluding Emeka's memory, said.

"Thank you. We have to tell the truth, sometimes, you know?" he replied, shaking her hand and swirling to the next person.

Emeka glimpsed her nod as though she had agreed with him before he said it. *Good thing we need to get everyone talking. But...* A thought seeped in. *What if they don't agree with me? What if, in their eyes, I am speaking gibberish? Making a Jordon point to butter up my pride?*

Emeka shook his head, his heart heavy with despair as though the world was crashing on him, as though all his public speaking had been vain, as if their motivation to fight corruption in the country were mere actions with no productive results. *I can't fail. Not now. Not ever!* He would take this fight to his grave if that was required of him.

Emeka snapped back to reality. He stared at the young lady, adorned in a white coat with a stethoscope clamped around her neck. Her radiant dark skin and neatly styled cornrows accentuated her beauty. A medical student. He smiled at her, an encouraging smile to keep her at ease.

Is she here to ask for assistance in her research?

Emeka muffled his chuckle with a cough. He couldn't remember studying medical science. Even the chemistry questions his teacher boasted he solved during his high school days when he was called to humiliate his senior, but he ended up embarrassing himself for his inability to tackle the question. More like his late father's persistent desire for him to study medical science, to become a doctor, but didn't they know his intelligence reigns within the scope of Art? To become one of the few professions that impact knowledge and shape the future of others?

"Prof, I'd like to speak with you privately," she whispered, her words frail as if afraid they would escape the sanctity of their privacy and be carried away by the restless whispers of the crowd.

Privately? Emeka, in nanosecond, wondered what was so confidential about whatever she wished to tell him that couldn't be uttered here.

I hope she isn't here to tell me to help her to persuade a lecturer to get her extra scores because it's a no for me if that's the case.

He nodded.

"Office sixty-eight."

Arms suddenly curled around Prof Emeka when he looked over at the owner, he chuckled. The dramatic Ifeoma, who didn't for once prefer the propriety of formality, unmasking to everyone the closeness of their relationship, beamed.

"You have an interview with me in three minutes. Please, be ready," she said, tugging him away from the buzzing congratulators.

They retreated to a secluded corner, away from prying eyes, for the interview. Emeka watched her in high esteem as she stuffed out a wireless microphone, handing it to him, which he tucked under his earlobe, connecting it to his lips. She positioned a camera at a little distance, ready to capture his every expression.

"Ready?" she asked, her demeanour now all

business, the intimacy between them temporarily eclipsed by their professional roles. It had always been like this: an interview after every public speaking session. "So, Prof Stanley, what do you say about the death of Mr. Ejike, who revealed the embezzlement of the current government?"

Emeka paused, allowing a pregnant silence to sprawl around them. Then he began to speak in a low, thoughtful cadence.

"Thank you for giving me this opportunity to air my opinion regarding the news circulating the net."

The atmosphere grew charged, like the calm before a storm.

"First, Mr. Ejike's action was heroic and courageous, creating room for protest and discussion. The government's laxity to human rights and its dereliction of duty to the law of the country should be condemned in all ramifications. They no longer care about public opinion or what the citizens think, and they seem to be forgetting that we're the same people who put them there."

"Do you mean we have to remove them? But how?"

"Removing them must be coordinated and done thoroughly, with no haste. We need voices, we need all hands on deck, and we can't achieve that if we remain silent. Mr. Ejike has taken courageous action, and it is incumbent upon us to follow in his footsteps. We must ensure that his demise is not in vain!" He spat out the last word with a rancorous disdain for the government, his words landing like poisoned darts. He noticed that Ifeoma winced.

Ifeoma recomposed herself, taking her time to ask the next question as though words had deserted her.

Then she asked; "I heard you delivered a speech for a call for action. What are your underlying themes?"

Emeka was amused at her abstinence to exclude herself from the hall even though she was present.

"Resistance and immunity. Being resistant creates a path for immunity to materialism, corruption, and bribery. These are the weapons the government uses against us, and we need people with a solid wall of resistance and immunity around them if we're to remove the current government from the seat.

As much as the earlier mentioned are important, knowledge shouldn't be overlooked and underestimated. Knowledge, they say, is power, but being in the wrong hands is destructive. We may need that destructive power (knowledge) if the government fails to amend their way. That's all I have to say. Thank you for hosting me."

"Thank you for your time, Prof Stanley."

He nodded, detaching the wireless microphone from his ear and handing it to Ifeoma, who, in turn, cast herself on him. He nearly staggered.

"You are so good, Prof."

"Oh please, your journalism skills still stun me. Keep up the work."

They strode to the nearest canteen and bought some snacks.

"See you later, dear." He waved at Ifeoma, who rotated in the direction of her faculty of mass communication. Emeka remembered how their relationship bloomed and how he met her as vividly as a painting in which every stroke is perfectly defined. Despite the graceful elegance and poise in which she moved as a swan, she'd appeared lost in his sight. Two green files were on her left hand, her shoes creaking beneath the tiled floor. She'd scuttled past him as her perfume was as ethereal as a cloud, light and airy, wrapping him in a celestial embrace.

"Excuse me, I think you're in the wrong corridor." Emeka watched her swirl, wide-eyed.

"Sorry…can I get the bursar office?" he loved her stuttering, her glaring shyness that made her face flushed.

He chuckled. "Clearly, you miss your way. Come with me, please. " He'd aided her, ensuring a smooth process of her registration until she started her semester lectures. Then, their relationship blossomed, and he assisted her in her academic research on journalism. She was the one who propelled him to engage in public speaking years ago, as well as lend a voice to the voiceless, ensuring that the citizens' voices and public opinion shouldn't be muffled.

Emeka sighted a figure huddled beside the door of his office, brows crinkled. He muttered an 'oh' as realization kicked him, the medical student who sought his attention earlier.

"Come in." He unblocked his office entrance, sauntering in, and the medical student trailed behind him. He seated, glancing at her properly.

"Have a seat, please."

"Thank you, Prof," she mumbled, siding on the wooden chair in front of his desk. "Sir, I have been following up on your public session and have been taking notes of your themes. You see, sir, the government has finally turned deaf ears to the cries of my community. A rampant outbreak of illness has ravaged my community after a devastating flood that nearly tore us apart. We need help. My community needs help."

KEPRESSNG

Emeka was silent, allowing her words to flow in a soft undertone. Her voice wavered, breaking intermittently. He placed his palms under his chin as though in deep meditation, in a deep reverie, but he was merely glancing at her, digesting her words. Then he sighed and sat upright.

A sudden ping buzzed around them. Emeka glanced at his phone to see a new notification. He used his thumb to swipe it open.

The headlines read: *Prof Emeka advocates a call for action in an interview with a mass communication student named Ifeoma, an aspiring journalist.*

The anonymous blogger again. Emeka was curious about who was behind the blog, the phenomenal ghost that already knew he'd had an interview with Ifeoma. Although he once suspected Ifeoma, he discarded the thoughts because Ifeoma would tell him if she was behind the blog.

A sudden slew of ideas whizzed through his mind. If the anonymous blogger he hadn't met could aid him in his quest to trample corruption and tackle government dereliction of duty, then whoever they were would be on his side. They'd be fighting the same cause. A cadet of the same-motivated fighters would give him a sense of direction. He gave the medical student a jaunty grin.

"I will consider your request if you're able to provide the identity of the face behind the Anonymous Sensation blog in three days' time."

Emeka noticed the student's her lip squeeze in a tight line. *Is she hesitating?* He shrugged at the thought.

"Thank you, Prof Stanley. I will do that," the student said, getting up.

Emeka nodded grimly.

"Don't worry. If you are unable to do so, we'll work something out. What's your name?"

"Amina Ejike."

"You're Igbo?" Emeka's brows creased.

At her nod, his eyes nearly pop out. "Oh my goodness, you're the daughter of Christopher Ejike, recently killed by the government?"

Emeka saw himself unconsciously hauling his hand over her shoulder, three strides to her, engulfing her in a brotherly hug. The man whose actions motivated him to speak up at the cruelty of the government.

The student nodded.

"I'm so sorry for your loss, Amina. Your father's death won't be in vain, I promise," he finally said.

He led her outside his office.

The propriety of the death threat letters, the redundancy of it, had begun to irritate Emeka, gnawing at his patience like a persistent mosquito buzzing in his ears. As he rounded up to the pavement of his three-bedroom apartment, where he saw the envelope tucked under his rug, he hissed. Couldn't they unveil their true identities so he could confront them?

The initial encounter had set his heart quivering, his palms dampened with fear and worry, as if the unseen claws of a grim reaper were tightening their grip on him. He had searched tirelessly, going door to door among his neighbours, seeking answers to the sender's identity, but each inquiry yielded negative results, further fuelling his anxious heart.

The second time wasn't much different from the first. Now he saw this as superfluous, an extrinsic action of a coward. He tore the letter after reading its contents. It was the usual 'We are watching you. Be careful.' To hell with this undercover 'detectivism'.

Emeka sank on his couch, unknotting his tie, shoving out his shoes simultaneously with his hands and draping over his suit jacket from his body afterwards. He culled his phone to read the anonymous blog post made about his interview with Ifeoma. The dictions was artful, practically highlighting the significance of taking action by using the idiom: 'a stitch in time, saves nine.'. From the sophisticated stylishness of sentences, Emeka could swear it must be written by a purposeful, obstinate woman who might have wanted to give the mute voice, lift the trampled, and strength to the weak. A smile crept across his face, and he eagerly anticipated meeting the mysterious blogger.

Na this kind of people I dey look for. Solid walls of resistance around them.

His phone wailed. He connected the call and leapt to his feet, dashing inside his room. "I almost forgot that today is the D-Day for the seminar. I will be there in a few minutes."

Being a professor isn't an easy job, oh, he mused.

The National Public Speakers Session (NPSS), which was held a week ago, invited Prof Emeka to their quarterly conference as a guest speaker on the theme: 'Recalcitrance and inexorable' had proven to be a big feast for him. It was a grand occasion for him, a chance to be seen and heard beyond the confines of his teaching institution.

Standing on the podium while his hands drummed repeatedly on the lectern, he waited for the murmuring to subside. It had been three hours since it began, and people still streamed in like a never-ending tide. The host, a tall young fellow who looked lethargic as though he had been suffering from lack of nourishment, signalled him to start speaking. Emeka cleared his throat and exhaled, accentuating his introduction almost in a whisper.

"I, Prof S. I. Emeka, in an uttermost gratitude to be standing before you, honourable ladies and gentlemen, for the theme of being inexorable in good deeds and to profess my opinions."

Emeka paused, brows furrowed at the movement stirring in the cluster of five orgulous-looking men. Then he saw a nozzle pointed at him. He gazed at the handler, at the unfamiliarity of his and his gang's expressionless faces. And blood drained from his face. His heart pounded. Emeka gripped the lectern tighter to steady his trembling hands. So, they finally take action? He knew right before he spoke that it would change everything.

"The government must be stopped."

Emeka's body froze like a fish out of water. At first, he felt nothing, then a searing sensation flared in his arm and sailed through his body. He belched out blood, and the room erupted in cacophony, people running helter-skelter, scampering for safety, nearly trampling each other on their way out. He tried to point at them but realized his shot arm couldn't lift - it dangled.

"Let's get him to the hospital. He's bleeding too much."

KEPRESSNG

Emeka saw himself being shoved from the lectern, away from the podium. He sighed at the dizziness engulfing him, and he let the darkness welcome him to its adobe.

Breaking news: Prof Emeka was shot at the NPSS last week. As we speak, he's battling for his life. More information about his well-being will be revealed soon. Stay calm!

Chaos erupted among students, lecturers, and his little followers.

Terror clawed at Ifeoma's spine as she bolted inside the media department. She had been here countless times with Prof to announce through the school media any upcoming sessions he had. Ifeoma panted, gasping.

"Please, make an announcement for them to gather at the hall."

The head of the media team nodded at her, understanding what she meant as recognition flickered in his eyes. They have to protest for the culprit to be found!

As Ifeoma bolted back, she contemplated whether to visit Prof In the hospital or ensure the success of the public session she intended to conduct. But will they attend? She wasn't Prof; they'd heed his call without protest. But this was his life they were talking about here, wasn't it? They had to attend.

She snapped out of her reverie as a hand grabbed her. Twirling to face its owner, Ifeoma stared down at the female whose eyes were filled with almost what made her heart swell with pride: she had the same fervour to fight and tackle corruption.

"I want to –"

"Come with me. There's no time."

The figure followed Ifeoma.

A memory flashed in her mind; the memory of her father's bruised face and battered body, blood siphoning from the slashes that zigzagged across his bare back. He was beaten for speaking up in his workplace as a civil servant over the embezzlement of money that his senior in rank had snooped over. Despite declining their bribe, they were determined to shut him up forever.

He barely survived each clandestine attack until a truck towed him over on his way from work. She'd sobbed, wailed, at how easily criminals roam free without receiving justice for their crimes. But where is justice when the freedom of fair hearing and expression had become treason, had been robbed, corrupted by the same leadership that should be protecting them?

Her father's death wouldn't be in vain. She'd fight to death if that's what it means.

Speak up! Fight or remain silent forever!

Ifeoma stood at the same podium that Prof Emeka had frequently graced with his presence during public speaking engagements, staring at the eyes glued on her. She knew Prof Stanley might not like her action, but it had to be done. They were, after all, fighting the same cause – the dereliction and malevolence of the government. She cleared her throat, adjusting her wireless microphone. Her voice would be heard nationwide, but her face would remain unseen.

"Days ago, Prof Stanley. I. Emeka was shot in his arm at the NPSS's conference, battling for his life as we speak. The culprit is yet to be found, proving to be a challenge, but we suspect it to be linked to the high-profile citizens hiding under the shadow of the government, allowing thugs to do their dirty jobs," she paused, mimicking Prof Emeka's mannerisms, roaming her eyes across the audience, ensuring they remained spellbound.

"While we can't wait for them to strike again, individuals have joined us to fight for deserved justice. Amina Ejike, please, come forward."

Ifeoma watched the medical student strut out, head held high. Amina had approached her days ago, after Prof Emeka was shot, pleading to join them in their fight. Ifeoma had requested any written article. And she felt a deep sympathy for the girl and her community. The scarcity of food, the slowness of water resources, and then a whirlwind of sickness. She was keen and unyielding in her quest to seek help for her community, and Ifeoma thought she might need more hands in their fight. To top it all, Amina Ejike had turned out to be the daughter of the man who motivated them to act.

Amina stood at the little lectern and began to speak immediately to the crowd as soon as she flung the book, she held open.

"The reluctance of the minister of health, the national health section, to provide adequate medical supplies to the community of Bori has been heard by me, and I must, in my capacity, do everything to have it solved. Look at the educational section; the lecturer's salary has been pending, yet they remain passionate about their job. Are we going to stay silent and allow this to go on? My father single-handedly and courageously prevented the national treasure from being slandered. Are we—"

Whispers of shock and disbelief rippled through the crowd, interrupting Amina's words. Everyone's attention was suddenly diverted to their phones, expressions of surprise etched upon their faces. Ifeoma shared glances with Amina and crinkled her brows.

Words like *'I can't believe this,'*, *'This is so surprising'*, *'So he be homo all this while. Chia!'*, *'Omo! My shock has been shocked.'* *'ah! This is disgusting!'*

Curiosity gripped Ifeoma, and she fished out her phone quickly, realizing it had been pinging with a new notification and a shocking headline: *'Prof Emeka is caught in bed with a man and is wanted by the government.'*

Ifeoma nearly flung her phone away. No, this can't be possible. Prof can't be gay. She looked around and noticed everyone was departing from the hall, still whispering.

"Come on, we need to see Prof before the police get him." She bolted out with Amina, dashing to the nearest bus stop, heading to the hospital where Prof Emeka was admitted.

The journey to the hospital felt agonizingly long for Ifeoma. She fidgeted in her seat, tempted to leap out of the moving vehicle and use her own two feet to hasten their progress. But she stayed calm, tugging at the hem of her dress. Sometimes, she would bite her lower lip.

When they reached their destination, Ifeoma shouted over her shoulder for Amina to pay the fare, running into the hospital.

Ifeoma got to the receptionist, a nurse huddled behind a cubicle, panting.

"I'd like to see the Prof that was admitted here days ago," she pleaded, her voice filled with urgency. This was her first time, and she had no time to waste. The nurse sluggishly opened a large book, lazily trailing her finger across its pages. Ifeoma felt a surge of impatience, yearning to prod the nurse into working faster.

Then the nurse glanced up, expressionless.

"There is only one hour left until the visiting period is over. Ward Thirty," the nurse monotoned.

Ifeoma nodded fervently, rushing towards the ward, catching the sound of hurried footsteps trailing behind her. She could sniff the stale smell of drugs, disinfectant and blood. Ifeoma paused at the door, taking a deep breath before entering. No one else was present in the room, but she could see that Prof Emeka was awake, his injured hand wrapped in white bandages, the other connected to an intravenous drip. Yet, his phone rested on his lap, and Ifeoma could only imagine that he had seen the damning news.

"Is it true?" she asked, her voice filled with a mix of uncertainty and concern, manoeuvring to his front, arms crossed.

"It is not me, please." His voice was frail but resolute. "I can't never do that. I don't know how I appeared in the video. This must be one of their ploys to get me down. Believe me, Ifeoma."

Ifeoma desperately wanted to believe him. She wanted to accept that the video was faux, a mere visual manipulation. But a visual image, especially one as real as this, was hard to ignore. She couldn't get over the moaning, the sound of thrusting, the plea for more.

She thought she saw a glimmer of tears. But when she gazed again, it was gone. Could it be possible that he was genuinely innocent?

"It is not true," a new voice chirped.

They turned to the door, and Amina Ejike and a superciliously haughty-looking young man in a brown tuxedo suit and sweatpants were sauntering in. He looked youthful, strands of hair lining his upper lip and beard that shrouded all of his jaw. But Ifeoma spotted a lawyer's scarf tucked beneath the books he held. A lawyer?

If there's a lawyer, that means the police are close. Fear clothed Ifeoma's spine, goosebumps spiking out of her skin. But Ifeoma crinkled her brows. *Why is he carrying a book like a journalist? Is he?* Ifeoma shook her head.

"What do you mean?" Ifeoma asked, sceptical.

"The video is real, but it's not Stanley. Read the latest news."

Her phone pinged with a new notification.

How did he know the news? Blogger?

Anonymous Sensation: The circulating video featuring the accused Prof Emeka, is genuine, but it doesn't depict him. The individual appearing in the video has come forward to explain the issue. Tune in to Wazobia FM, 91.5, in three seconds.

Ifeoma swiftly activated her phone radio, and a resonating voice eerily resembling Prof Emeka's spoke through; she would have thought it was him if not that Prof lay feebly on the bed in front of her.

"Hello, thank you for honouring our call to speak up regarding the trending video. Can you tell us what you know?" Ifeoma heard a female voice from the background. There was a murmur, and a baritone voice blared, sounding annoyed - perhaps, angered.

"By the gods, I never expected to become a sensation upon my return from the United States. I stumbled upon a video featuring me and a male gigolo, and I must confess, I am accountable for my indiscretion. It was my own fault, a lapse in judgment. Weeks ago, I visited a local club where a young gigolo propositioned me for a night of pleasure. Succumbing to temptation, I indulged, for I cannot suppress my desires. Oh, my dear, I am proudly bisexual, and I couldn't care less about society's judgments.

To shorten the tale, I have been on a quest to unearth my long-lost family, whom I haven't seen in ages. I had heard whispers about the accused Prof, who apparently bears a resemblance to me, leading me to suspect that he might be my twin. If my intuition is correct, my apologies, dear brother, for this unsavoury appearance. As for the gigolo, I shall locate him and those responsible for orchestrating this sordid affair.

Lastly, the Navigo government, seeking the apprehension of the accused Prof, will first have to face me in court before laying a finger on him. Let us resolve this matter definitively," the voice waned.

The room plunged into a tense silence. They turned at the stranger with them.

"Meet Barr Akachi Kingsley. The face behind the Anonymous Sensation blog. He's the one who contacted the alleged twin of Prof Stanley and the lawyer who will be defending him," Amina stated, unveiling the enigmatic figure standing before them.

"How did…you…" Emeka stuttered. Ifeoma nodded in support.

"Get all the information posted online? I have a media team, students and lecturers alike, that monitored major events until the wisp of Prof Emeka's fervour to fight corruption got my interest. I included him in my list of people I lean to expand their voice to a wide range."

Soldiered feet resonated as eyes darted to the door. The police must be here to take him away.

"Don't worry, to fight is to choose not to remain silent forever."

IKECHUKWU HENRY is a Nigerian Ìgbo writer and a student who loves to explore the adversities and darkness of the human mind and his surroundings. Along with his fervour for books, his hobbies include reading, surfing websites for Kdrama/Cdrama movies, and browsing the latest magazines to submit to. He's a myth enthusiast, and when he's less busy, he can be found beta reading for writers.

He was the Ro-novella Writing contest First Edition 2022 first runner-up and was longlisted for the Sevhage Prize For Short Fiction 2023. His works have appeared in Kahalari Review, Afrihill Press, Swim Press, The AfterPast Review, Icreative Review, Synchronized Chaos and others.

DUMB LUCK
- Daniel Alaka

No one else was home when Zara killed her mistress. It was quite lucky for her.

Oga would have been home that morning had his flight not been delayed inexplicably. Twice.

The twins - Rehoboth and Deborah - would have been home that morning if they had not been sleeping over at their aunt's place in Ajah. The crude, voluptuous woman had burst in the afternoon before to take them away. Zara wasn't sure she had planned it with Madam beforehand.

The six-gun wouldn't have even been a factor had someone not thrown the thing through the window of the shack Zara shared with the gateman – who would have been available had he not stolen off into the night after news of his son's untimely death two days before. The thud as it hit the ground had woken her up.

Madam was being a self-righteous bitch, as per usual.
BANG!

KEPRESSNG

The silence made everything much louder. The faint buzzing of electronics – like the fridge in the kitchen - the whirring of the standing fan blew frigid air on and away from the two occupants of the living room. Oddly enough, even the television, on mute, tore through the stillness like tissue paper.

Her ears were still ringing. The way her hands shook, it was a wonder she could hold on to the gun – hot as it was. She'd slumped onto an armchair – the one adjacent to the TV, where she was forbidden from sitting – and was staring straight at her mistress, who'd also slumped into an armchair. There was blood all over the sofa – Madam's head was leaking all over it – that Zara was compelled to clean. Almost. Madam's hollowed eyes stared back at her; the latent rage she was in when the bullet hit her skull manifested into an ugly scowl she'd take to the next world. Hanging awkwardly out of her hand was a leather whip, bought three years ago at about five thousand naira on the day Zara came from her home to work here. For her, specifically.

Zara was thirteen. She wanted to scream but couldn't quite get the sound out. She hadn't made one in thirteen years.

I've done an evil thing. Zara thought.
No, you haven't. Her thoughts replied.
Joy. Terror. Guilt. Glee. Confusion. Sadness.
The ringing in her ears.
BANG!

She had a headache. She needed to eat.
Can I eat, ma? Zara thought. She looked to her mistress, putting her hand to her mouth so she would understand. Madam said nothing. The work wasn't done yet, so she wasn't sure if she should or shouldn't.

KEPRESSNG

The fan came for her again. She shivered under the sweater she wore every day to cover the scars.

Looking in from the outside, one might make the mistake of thinking Zara is evil, though she would consider herself far from that. The calm stemmed more from indecision than anything else.

She could get up, but what would she do after that?

She could drop the gun, but what would she do after that?

She could pray, but what would she do after that?

She could run away – the best course of action – but what would she do after that?

No! This isn't what I wanted! I didn't want to kill Madam!

Didn't I?

I didn't! I swear!

You did. I did. I wanted to kill her.

There was a creak. Zara sat upright and turned to the door. Nothing happened. The creaking remained, but nobody came in.

Stupid rats. She thought. Madam had asked her to kill them before. Zara sank deeper into the chair and laughed.

A news show was on the television; a man and a woman were talking about something. It was on mute, so she couldn't hear them.

BANG!

It still rang in her ears. She could barely hear anything but her own thoughts. No one was coming.

No one was around.

Ma. Can I be watching the TV, Ma?

She expected a "No", like she always got. She wasn't allowed to watch the TV, like she wasn't allowed to go to school, even though her mother was promised that she would do the latter. "You're here to work, Zara, not do stupid things like that! Now go and wash the plates! After that, you'll pick the twins up from school! Dumb idiot!"

Now, all she got was a dead stare.

No one heard. She realised. *No one is coming.*

She laughed again. No one heard.

She reached over for the remote, which was on the glass table before her. She did it slowly, eyeing Madam and the whip in her hand. She could still feel it. The ringing in her ears. She took the remote and winced. Nothing happened.

Thank you, Ma, she mouthed.

When Zara was six years old, still living with her mother and many brothers and sisters, and yet to speak her first words, her Uncle Rashid – in a moment of rage-filled candour – told her that God didn't exist.

Through the years, Zara had learnt not to judge her uncle too harshly. In the space of half a year, pests had taken his crops, the rains had taken his home, disease had taken his wife, and a mad cow had taken his children. At the time, he found himself pouring all his frustrations on his young niece; the clothes on his back weren't even his own.

Having gone from poor to destitute in a matter of months, it was clear that God wasn't smiling at him. That was probably hard for him to accept. It was more likely that God just wasn't there at all than that he was there, allowing adversity to befall and overcome him. It was easier as Zara grew to understand why he said what he said. But at age six, when she barely understood that life was unfair, it had been the strangest thing she had heard. And it was wrong – she had known that even if she knew nothing else.

Later that night, she tried to tell her mother what Uncle Rashid had said.

Mummy. Is God not real? Tell Uncle Rashid that God is real, like you told me, now, she had mouthed. But nobody heard. Maybe that was why Uncle Rashid had told her in the first place.

The next morning, Zara's older sister, Zuweira, told their mother – quite innocently - what Uncle Rashid said. She had overheard when she was coming back from the stream but had forgotten about it completely. Their mother didn't forget, though. She went out and returned later with many angry, shouting people. They grabbed Uncle Rashid, who didn't understand what was going on, and took him away.

The morning after that, Zara and her siblings were told that Uncle Rashid was dead.

Good. Zara had thought. *He deserved it.*

A year after that, Zara's mother caught her stealing meat from the cooking pot. Irate, her mother sent her to kneel down and raise her hands in her room, promising to beat her severely before going out to the market. She was not allowed to go and play with the other children in the village.

When her mother returned, she had calmed down significantly. She seemed to have forgotten about Zara's little crime and instead just sent her out of the room. It was a day later that Zara learnt that the children who went out to play were kidnapped.

Usually, when she took meat from the pot, no one ever caught her.

There was a time she had dropped the cover, and it hit the ground with a startling crash. She had frozen, almost expecting to be caught, but no one came; two of Zara's aunties were having a shouting match outside, and everyone had gone to break them up or watch them go at it.

Another time, when she was ten, some large boys tried to rob her when she was going to the market. When she refused to give them her money, they surrounded her and threatened to kill her. She didn't know if they would have or not. She couldn't scream for help, so she picked up a small stone and threw it at the largest boy. She missed.

"You unfortunate girl!" The leader of the gang had said. "We were just trying to scare you before. Now we're going to kill you."

She believed him when she saw the first knife. But almost immediately, somebody called out.

"Hey! What's going on there?!"

The boys – startled – turned and ran away, leaving little Zara alone with the tall, ugly man who had yelled. The man walked her to the market and back home, and he rubbed the bump on his head every step of the way.

The leader of the boys had called her an unfortunate girl. Her last memory of her father was him calling her the same thing. She didn't believe either of them, the same way she didn't believe her Uncle Rashid before they killed him.

God was real. And every day, he smiled at her.

So, when the strange woman came to her mother - promising that one of her children would be able to go to school and earn money if they came to Lagos with her - and her mother had volunteered the unfortunate mute that no one seemed to care for, she hadn't been afraid to go. She'd been excited, even.

Zara turned the TV off after three hours. The remote was still in her hand, as was the gun. She needed to go back home. That was the only place she would be safe. She would tell her mother that she wasn't allowed to go to school and that she was beaten and mistreated, among other things. Madam couldn't stop her from leaving anymore.

She didn't remember how to get home, of course. She wasn't sure she even really knew where her home was. But she knew who would know.

She didn't know where that person lived either, but she knew she would find him.

First, Zara went out to the shack, where she slept with the gateman. Madam didn't want her in the house, though she never said why. It was never important anyway. Months from now, she would have bigger things to worry about and would even forget how the place looked. She didn't need to remember it anyway, as she didn't have much to take from it. Only two skirts and two long-sleeved shirts. A pair of slippers. She didn't even have a phone. "Who do you want to be calling? Someone who can't even speak! Get out, jare!"

She put all her clothes in a small bag. The bag belonged to the old gateman, but Zara figured he wouldn't mind. He'd always been kind to her. She put the gun in the bag as well. She wasn't sure why, but she knew she would need it later. At least it made her feel safe.

Next, she took the bag, barely full, back to the house. She headed straight for Madam and Oga's room, where Madam kept her handbags and purses and where Madam kept her money. It was a lot of money, much more than she had ever been allowed to handle or even count before. She looked around the room, but she didn't see much more. It didn't matter. What she had would be enough.

There was a dress in one of Madam's drawers. It had many colours – red, blue, green and others. It was like the rainbow she had seen once at home. It was beautiful. And she had never seen Madam wear it before. There were many things here she had never seen Madam wear. It had no sleeves, and it was much too long for her. She had never owned anything like it before. And now it was hers.

Her stomach rumbled. She still hadn't eaten, she realised. She hadn't eaten since the morning before. She needed to eat before she went home.

What was the last thing I made for the twins, now? Toast. Toast sandwich. Madam said I shouldn't eat with them. Madam said I shouldn't eat. I ate normal bread....

Some minutes passed, and Zara had finished eating the best meal she had taken in a while. Probably in her whole life, even at home, she hadn't had an entire fridge at her disposal. Still, no one had arrived. Somewhere in Abuja, Oga was yelling at the flustered airport security over a flight yet again delayed. She was wearing Madam's dress now – the rainbow one – and she had a purple scarf wrapped around her hair – also stolen from Madam's things. It surprised her how well the dress fit – it was still quite big, even after reducing the length with scissors so she could walk properly. The dress was sleeveless, so she could see the scars she'd accumulated over three years.

She'd never felt so beautiful.

Zara had many brothers and many sisters. A big family, albeit a poor one. So it wasn't much of a loss when the woman from Lagos came and took her away to work.

"Your children cannot make something of themselves here." The woman had told her mother. "Especially not your daughters. If they come to Lagos, I'll give them good work where they can earn good money and even go to school, on top."

Zara's father had died not too long before. He'd been struck by lightning, and the family – for understandable reasons – blamed Zara. For her part, Zara never mourned his death. Some members of her family – her mother included – thought she just didn't understand what had happened, even though she had seen some of her cousins die before.

In a way, it was good fortune for everyone involved. Zara's family could get rid of her for good, and Zara could leave the village for good. And she was supposed to benefit from it too, so in a way, they were doing her favour.

The day she was to go off, nobody bid her goodbye. Her mother gave her a bag with food in it and said a brief prayer for her safety. Then, she hurried inside like a ghost was chasing her. That was very early in the morning, and Zara looked at the woman who had now taken ownership of her. Whether it was for support, guidance, or even an explanation, it didn't matter because neither could be found in the woman's scowl.

"Come! And walk quickly if you don't want me to slap your head!" The woman barked, and Zara followed her into the dawn.

The journey to Lagos was a long one that involved a lot of bus rides, a lot of walking, and a lot of sleeping in between. The woman had slapped Zara a couple of times for reasons ranging from being too slow and fast, not answering when she was called, not reminding her she couldn't speak, and just being annoyed. The last time she felt the sting at the back of her head, she was being woken up to see their final destination.

"This is Lagos," the woman announced. "Not your village. You can't survive here if you don't work. And you must work, you hear?"

The woman continued to talk, and Zara had barely listened. She'd been dreaming of Hauwa. Again. She wasn't sure if she was happy to be woken up.

The doorbell rang.

"Zara! You stupid girl! Is that you? Open this door quickly, now!"

It was Aunty Cass, Madam's friend from next door. She could recognize the shrill voice from anywhere, and it cut through her daydreams as it had many times before. Zara bolted to her feet and hurried to the door, where a short woman was waiting. She was wearing an Adire gown and a perpetual scowl, as she did anytime Zara saw her. Zara moved to kneel by way of greeting.

"What is that ugly thing you're wearing?! Do you think this is your father's house?!"

Zara looked down at her new dress. She shook her head.

Aunty Cass opened her mouth to say something but stopped herself. She was prone to forgetting that Zara couldn't speak and would instinctively try to scold her for her silence. Zara sometimes wondered if having to be considerate in such a small way made the woman hate her more. "Look, I don't have your time right now." Aunty Cass said impatiently. "Let me inside. I want to see your Madam!"

KEPRESSNG

Without giving Zara a moment to respond, she made to enter the house. Zara, in a panic, pushed her back. Aunty Cass stumbled a bit, nearly falling over. She looked at Zara, genuine confusion replacing her initial irritation and giving way to ire.

"Are you mad?" she screamed. "I said I want to see your Madam; you now want to kill me?!"

Zara shook her head.

"You don't want to kill me?!"

She shook her head again. She pointed to the inside of the house.

"You won't let me in?!"

She nodded.

"Why?!"

Zara rested her hands on her open palm and closed her eyes.

"She's sleeping?!"

She nodded.

"At twelve in the afternoon?!"

Zara paused. She hadn't realized it was so late. She nodded anyway.

"So... so that's why you want to injure me?!" Aunty Cass said, still incredulous.

Zara knelt a bit and made a praying gesture with her hands, looking as sorry as she could.

"Sorry for yourself! Let me inside and wake her up! I need to see her this morning!" Aunty Cass said. She made no move, however, as if afraid that Zara would shove her again. Zara simply shook her head.

"I said, 'let me in', now!"

She shook her head again, more vigorously.

"Did she say no one should enter the house while she's sleeping?!"

A pause. Then a nod. Then a hiss.

KEPRESSNG

"Okay, I'll wait outside. Go and wake up, Madam, sha. I don't know why someone will still be sleeping at this time. Go quickly! I need to speak to her now-now! And if I find out that Madam didn't tell you this thing, you stupid girl, I will cane you myself!"

The last thing Zara heard when she closed the door was a disgusting hiss. *Stupid woman.* She thought.

She considered telling the woman that Madam didn't want to see her. *No, Aunty Cass is stupid. She'll just enter like that.* No. She couldn't wait her out either. She needed to leave immediately.

She went to get her bag. The plates she used for her breakfast were still on the table, and the dishes in the sink still weren't washed. She didn't have the time. She couldn't even take any more valuable things. All she managed to do was remove the gun from her bag and stuff it in again at the bottom, under her clothes. She didn't notice the hole in the bag. She slung the bag over her shoulder and hurried out the backdoor in the kitchen.

The compound was empty. She rushed out from behind the house to the shack she shared with the gateman. She looked back to the house to see if Aunty Cass had seen her. She hadn't. She wasn't even there. Zara thought nothing of it until she heard the scream.

"JESUS!"

Zara headed out of the gate and ran into the street.

Hauwa was Zara's younger sister. Her mother said she was the most beautiful girl in the world. She was eleven years old when she died. She lived on in Zara's dreams, though.

Usually, she would sit in a tall chair and look down at Zara, who stood in front of her. She wore the same shirt and skirt she wore that day. Her slippers were lost in the river.

She was a happy child in life. She never smiled in her dreams.

"It's your fault." Hauwa would always say.

Zara would say nothing.

"Daddy died. I died. It's because of you."

Still Zara would say nothing.

Hauwa's a beautiful child. With her big eyes, her smile, and her long hair. The most beautiful girl in the village. Mama would say it every day.

"You killed us!" she would scream, and Zara would shake her head.

"You let us die! You let me die! I'd be alive because of you!"

Zara would shrug.

And it would continue like this again, and again, and again. Then Madam would scream Zara's name. Then, Madam would beat Zara again.

There was a supermarket at the end of the street of the one Madam lived in called Glory Mall, where Zara stopped to buy some chocolate to eat. She had only had some once, last Christmas, when it was being shared at the church's Christmas party. She dumped five bars of different chocolate brands on the cashier's table. After scanning her things, the cashier had asked Zara – with great concern – about the scars on her arm. Fortunately, the customer behind her started to complain that they were taking too much time and that she was in a hurry, so Zara was able to escape.

This was the farthest Madam had ever allowed her to go. The second she stepped out into the main street, she was lost.

They called him Uncle Lateef. He was from her hometown but lived here in Lagos. He visited regularly, though, and would bring gifts of clothes and food to the children when he came. She had met him once, in the Glory Mall. He told her that he was living somewhere called 'Ilorin Street' and that she could see him whenever she wanted to see her family for the holidays. She had never taken him up on the offer – partly because Madam would never even let her ask and partly because she wasn't interested in seeing her family again. She didn't hate them, but there was nothing for her there at the time.

Of course, there was nothing for her here as well, so she might as well go back.

The streets were beginning to look the same. The same badly tarred roads covered with litter. The same rotten gutters. The same cars parked by the side. The same nice houses hidden behind tall walls with pieces of glass stuck to the top. *I'm walking round and round.* The roads were mostly deserted, which she liked, save for one or two people who took little notice of her.

One woman stopped to stare at her with a pitiful look in her eyes.

She continued walking.

It was the middle of the afternoon. A very hot day. She was beginning to sweat. She was glad she hadn't worn her long-sleeved shirts like she always did. She was always boiling when she went out to buy things for Madam. She fell ill one time. She couldn't do any work for two days because of it. She enjoyed it very much. When she got better, though, Madam made her work twice as hard.

She stopped to rest on a bench by the side of the

road, placing her bag on the ground next to her. She stretched her legs out as she sat and started to eat her chocolates. The road on this street was less smooth. Every car passing by moved slowly. Some of the houses didn't have gates or even walls to hide behind. There were quite a few people walking past now. A woman with some loads on her head. Two young boys, one who was holding a football. A large street dog was sniffing around for scraps. Zara gave it some of her chocolate. It ate it up happily and went off to where it would die later that night.

She was halfway through her third chocolate bar when a man approached her. A heavy-looking man with a bald head. She kept eating. He gave her a sinister smile.

"Fine girl." He said. "I never see you before, o. Wetin carry you come this side?"

Zara didn't answer. Some seconds passed in silence. Another man started to approach from her left, looking more unkempt than the first.

"Ahn-ahn? We dey fight? You dey beef me? Answer na."

She still said nothing. She put her hand to her mouth and shook her head.

"Bossman, I no think she sabi talk o," a third man said, as he came in from her right side. She was surrounded before she knew it.

"Ah! Talk true!" the bald man exclaimed. He wore a look of concern that seemed genuine. "The devil is a liar. This fine girl? This life no balance at all."

The man shook his head while the others muttered in agreement. Zara simply finished her chocolate bar and pulled out a new one, holding her bag closer to her as she did so.

KEPRESSNG

"Heya, sorry about that, dear," the bald man said. "You can hear me, sha? Can't you?"

Zara nodded. She tore open the bar of chocolate and took a bite.

"This your chocolate nice, o," the man said. "Abi, you go give me small?"

He held out his hand humbly. Zara reluctantly put the entire thing in his hand. He snatched it away greedily.

"Ahn-ahn! Everything?! Thank you." His voice was sweet and snake-like. He took two bites of the chocolate bar. "And this chocolate nice, o. Where your mama? Your mama must be a rich woman o, if she fit buy this kind chocolate for you."

Zara grabbed her bag and tried to stand up. The man held out his hand and snatched the bag off her shoulder so smoothly she almost didn't notice it. Nobody noticed what fell out of the bag as he did so. Zara moved to take her bag back, but the man to her left grabbed her arm and held her back. The bald man started to scavenge through the bag.

"Na wa o. This girl na thief, o. Na so small girl go get money like this?"

"Make I see, Boss. Make I see," one of his lackeys begged. The man got a peek at the money in her bag, and his eyes widened with shock and greed. "Talk true. Na thief girl be this." He laughed. The bald man laughed with him. All the men laughed.

Zara didn't find it very funny. She scrambled herself out of the grip of the man who held her hands and rushed to the bald man holding her bag, hitting him as hard as she could in the stomach. It wasn't very hard, but it knocked the wind out of him for a while. The second man, moving quickly, cuffed her over the side of her head and pushed her off her feet. The sand felt coarse in her mouth. It took her a few seconds to find herself again, and that was when she saw it.

The three men stood above her laughing. The bald man took another bite from the chocolate bar.

"You're just unfortunate, you this girl. So you're stealing money at your age, and you want to start fighting on top?" He said, laughing with his mouth full. "Boys, help me, make we arrange this one. Since she wants to be unfortunate."

The bald man reached down with his free hand and grabbed Zara with her scarf.

BANG!

Click.

BANG!

Click.

Madam didn't know when she died. She didn't know when the bullet hit her skull, and she probably didn't even notice when Zara was holding the gun. Madam never paid attention to what Zara was doing when she was in a mood because what if she found herself pitying the house girl. If she had been paying, she'd noticed the gun had been with her when she started screaming. Something about clothes not being washed. Rushing into the living room, whip already in hand, screaming insults and a few obscenities.

BANG!

The gun in her hand was hot again. Her ears were ringing again as well, though not as badly as before. The half-opened chocolate bar was on the ground, caked with dust.

Zara got to her feet and brushed the dust off her dress. The bald man had a hole in his head, and one of his friends had one in his chest. Zara noticed the last one scrambling away, dragging himself across the ground with his hands. His hole was in his foot. She could hear him crying. She could hear the gun click.

It didn't take her very long to catch up and stomp on his hand so he would stop moving. He screamed and turned over on his back. He looked up to a gun barrel. A faint wet patch formed in his shorts. He was sweating. He was crying. His eyes looked past the gun and to the girl, begging her for his life.

"Please. Madam. I'm sorry, please. Please…"

Please, Madam. I'm begging. Please! Please! No! Stop! Please….

Zara winced.

BANG!

Click.

The man winced. He let out a squeal, something similar to how Zara imagined she would sound. She pulled the trigger again.

Click.

Fast forward a few months, Zara would be lying down exhausted in an abandoned car, looking back at this moment. Thinking how lucky it was that the man did not die. However, that was the future. In the present, Zara was disappointed. She watched him cry, spitting on him for good measure, and turned to get her bag. She noticed that people were starting to crowd the street, wondering who was shooting who. She needed to leave as quickly as possible.

"Zara! Is that you?!"

She hadn't gone too far when she heard her name and the frantic honking of a car.

"Zara! What are you doing here?! Where's your madam?!"

KEPRESSNG

Behind her – at a crossroads - a small car had pulled up at the side of the street. The driver's window was rolled down, and the driver was calling out to her to come and greet him. She knew the voice, and she knew the face. Uncle Lateef.

"Ha Zara, get in, get in!"

There's a river just outside Zara's home town. Every morning, Zara and her sisters would go there to fetch water with the other children. And every afternoon, Zara and her sisters would go there and play with the other children. Her brothers would be working at that time.

It's a big, large, long river with many twists and turns. At a certain point, the river drops off into a small valley, crashing through rocks, large and small as it does so. The end of the river remains unexplored, as the adults are afraid of the waterfall, and the children are told never to go there to play.

Some days, when they were bored, Hauwa and Zara would go to the waterfalls to play.

Zara was Hauwa's favourite sister. She loved to talk, and all Zara could do was listen, so, in theory, they were the perfect pair. They ventured out to that part of the river by accident, looking for a spot to fetch water away from the others who crowded the best parts of the river. Seeing it was the first time Zara remembered her sister being speechless.

The place Uncle Lateef lived in was smaller than she imagined. During those times he came to give nice gifts to them in the village, she always imagined that he lived in a house as big as a castle or something like the mosque that their family went to every Friday.

By the time I get home, mummy and them will be at the mosque.

She also imagined that he lived in a place like Madam's house – a place that was too big for one person to clean, sweep, and go around.

Of course, the place he lived was a big house, kind of like Madam's own. But when they got out of his car, he led her to the side of the house, to a small door that she would never have noticed if he hadn't shown it to her. He opened the door to what could only be described as a room.

That was where Uncle Lateef lived. A small room that had nothing but a large mattress on the floor, a small television on the wall across from it, and a wardrobe on the wall that had some clothes inside. There was another door, half opened, where Zara saw a toilet that hadn't been cleaned. There wasn't even a kitchen.

"Okay, Zara. You can sit over there." Uncle Lateef said, pointing to the mattress. "Put your bag anywhere you like. Let me quickly buy food for you. You want rice and beans?"

Zara nodded. Uncle Lateef smiled and left. He came back in shortly after.

"Should I turn the TV on?" he asked. He did it anyway, even before she nodded and walked out again.

There was music on the television – women dancing and men singing and throwing money around. Zara paid no attention to it. It was like those music shows that Deborah watched even though Madam didn't allow her to. She ignored those also.

I'm evil. I killed again.

No. You're not.
I did.
No.

She could see his eyes. The way the man begged for mercy with his tears, struck dumb with terror.

Please, Madam! Please! I'm begging you! I beg! Please! I'll...I'll... Ma, please! Please!...

Zara found herself touching the scars. They were hard – forming sturdy plateaus all about her tender skin. She wondered if she was now bulletproof.

She could see his eyes. She was happy.

When Uncle Lateef came in with the food, she changed the channel to a cartoon program. She wasn't paying much attention to that either. He had brought rice and beans, as he promised, with two pieces of meat on top, basted in an oily stew. It was nowhere near the feast she had taken earlier, but she smiled her thanks regardless. As she ate, Uncle Lateef asked her where she was headed.

"Home." She mouthed. She pointed in the general direction of her home – a random direction, that is.

"You wan go back home?" Uncle Lateef asked after a moment of confusion.

Zara nodded.

"That one na problem. I'm not going back until the holiday period. I don't have the money now."

Zara shook her head.

"I don't, o. You should have asked your Madam to call me since. I'm not going anywhere anytime soon."

Zara pointed to herself.

"You want to go by yourself?"

Zara nodded.

He shook his head. "No, o. A small girl like you? I can't let you take that journey by yourself."

Zara begged.

"I can't. No. I can't." Lateef asserted. He got to his feet as if the thought itself had stung him. "The road is dangerous these days if you don't know. If anything happens to you, what will I now tell your mother?"

She won't care. You won't even know.

"No. You're not going by yourself. That's the last word, okay? That's that," Lateef said. Zara didn't bother trying to argue.

Uncle Lateef said nothing else, though he seemed uneasy now. He checked the time on his phone. "Ah! It's four-thirty!" He said. "I'm almost late!"

As he headed out, he said to Zara. "I'm going to the Island for a meeting. I'll come back late at night. I'm going to lock the door. Tomorrow, I'll take you back to your Madam."

He punctuated his instruction by slamming the door, and true to his word, Zara heard the lock catch. She looked around the room again. It was much bigger than the room Madam locked her in sometimes and was lit too. She was glad.

The lights went off.

It still wasn't as dark.

Zara covered the food – *I'll eat it later in the evening* – and busied herself by looking around. There wasn't much to look around in, except the room with the toilet and the wardrobe. The room with the toilet was smaller than she thought, with a single shower head and a wash basin as the sole companions to the dirt-covered toilet. She considered helping him clean it. A towel and a sponge hung on the shower head. A single window opposite the wash basin, high up the wall. The bathroom wasn't nearly as nice as the four at her Madam's – that's one for each bedroom, including the guest room. She usually went outside in a small latrine that the gateman used.

The gateman would miss his bag. He would see his missing bag, find that Madam was dead, and curse Zara's name. It won't work.

She searched the wardrobe next. She saw some money – hundred and fifties – and took them all. A small phone with buttons and a black and white screen. Full battery. No sim card. She took it as well. A piece of paper, from a sticky note, next to a pen, with the words "Bus Stop Ido – Benson" written in the pen's red ink. She took the paper but left the pen.

She sat down and counted her money. Five hundred and fifty naira altogether. She put it in the bag along with the phone. Her hand brushed something cold. She pulled out the gun and put it on the bed.

Doesn't mummy care?

Nobody cares.

She remembered her brothers and sisters. Zuweira. Habib. Zainab, Ismail, Jibril. The others. She would show them the gun. The younger ones. She'll tell them the story about how she escaped, how she was now a killer. They'd be afraid of her. She had never scared anyone before today. She remembered the way the man looked at her. Maybe her mother would look at her the same way.

Maybe I'll tell them what happened to Hauwa.

She laughed. She didn't finish the food like she planned to.

It rained the day Hauwa died.

Zara didn't want to go there that day. Hauwa could tell. And she made her go anyway. They sat on the grass next to the rapids. Hauwa started talking about a boy who had begun to notice her in the market. Zara's attention was on the water. It was ferocious today. More than usual.

"You're not listening," Hauwa said. The clouds had started to form by then.

Let's go home!

"Not yet, Zara. Let's talk," Hauwa begged. "Please? If we go home now, Mama won't let us back outside. We'll be doing housework, and I won't be able to talk to you. And I haven't finished yet."

The first drop of rain. Then, the second. Then, the third. That third one hit Zara square on the nose. In the distance, there was thunder.

BANG!

Don't finish! We need to go now!

"Okay, then," Hauwa said, getting to her feet. "We can go..."

The rain was getting heavier now. Zara was getting up as well. She looked down, making sure she was well-balanced as she stood up. When she looked up again, her sister was running towards the water.

BANG!

Hauwa!

The sky opened. The world was blue with lightning. Zara bolted after her sister.

Hauwa climbed on one of the rocks just as Zara reached her. She stuck her tongue out, first to taunt her sister, then to spit out the rainwater.

"If you want to go, you have to get me down first!"

BANG!

Get down from there!

Hauwa stuck her tongue out again.

With no other options, Zara started climbing the rock her sister was on. She succeeded despite the rain and the way it made the stone slippery and muddy. But once she got to the top, her sister was no longer there. She had jumped on the other rock.

BANG!

Zara could see her with half-closed eyes through her hair and the rainwater.

"Let's see what's on the other side!" Hauwa laughed. "Maybe we can find a new village!"

This isn't the time for this!

BANG!

She tried to move forward, but she couldn't. She didn't want to slip. The waters raged under the feet. The waters raged above her head. Around her, the waters raged. And through it all, Hauwa giggled.

God... help us.

BANG!

The world turned dark for a split second. Then, white light. Then, a scream. Then, the thunder. Both rang in Zara's ears. She didn't expect to see her sister when she opened her eyes.

It was still dark when she awoke. Darker even. She knew it was morning.

Her stomach was hurting. It had hurt her, even in her dream where she shot Madam again, as well as Aunty Cass. This time, they were both begging her for life.

BANG!

She shot up from the bed, spilling the now sour rice and beans on the ground and bolted to the toilet. That was dark as well. She sat there in the darkness, sweating. She felt ill. Her stomach fought her. It was angry. She couldn't fight back. She came close to making her first sound ever. She didn't hear the footsteps outside.

Her stomach settled eventually, and she flushed. She stayed on the toilet, though. Something made her feel weak. It wasn't the food, she knew.

She needed to leave.

"Bro, I can't lie to you. I saw it with my own eyes."

"A gun? On your bed? E wo!"

The first voice belonged to Uncle Lateef. It put her on alert. She had never heard the other voice before, though he spoke as if he knew Uncle Lateef well. The two of them spoke in hushed tones, and Uncle Lateef sounded quite fearful.

"I heard it on the radio. The girl killed her, Madam, and I think she shot four other guys in that area."

"Ah! That one loud o."

A moment of silence, save for the shuffling of feet as Uncle Lateef paced. Zara didn't see that his hands were on his head or that he was asking under his breath who he had offended.

"And I allowed this girl inside my car o!" he lamented. "The bastard is sleeping on my bed right now! With gun! I bought her food!"

His friend groaned and hissed, "When you won't listen to news…"

"What nonsense are you saying? There's a killer in my room, you're telling me about news!"

"Isn't it from radio news that I told you about her?!" the friend shouted.

"Shhhh! Keep quiet!"

"Okay, make I stop listening to radio, na! That's how they go implicate you for robbery next time. Idiot!"

"Shhhh!" Uncle Lateef said again, in a louder

whisper. "You'll wake her up!"

Another silence, this time without the pacing.

"Okay," the friend said, "Okay. Okay. Here's what we'll do... Do you have the gun?"

"No o. I left it with her. I just looked at her and locked the door," Uncle Lateef replied. "Or should I..."

"No, it's okay. It's good you didn't touch anything. Don't worry. And you're sure the door is locked."

"Yes."

"You're sure?"

"Yes, na."

"I don't want to hear story, o. We're going to bring police, so before anyhow anyhow go occur..."

"My loc

k full ground, na. You know. You know."

"Okay," the friends said, finally sounding satisfied. "Now, quickly while she's sleeping."

"I hope we won't see anyhow sha."

"They'll just come and bundle her away. No wahala. Nothing go spoil. So far you go meet them, them no come meet you. That's when wahala go burst. And that one, you go give me space: I don't know you, bruv."

"Bastard."

Zara got up from the toilet when their laughter receded. She grabbed her bag and put the gun inside. It was empty. It wouldn't protect her from the people that were coming. And they would take her away and kill her, like the angry men wanted to do the day before. She remembered Uncle Rashid.

"Zara! Zara, I'm scared."

God was real. And if He likes you well enough, if you're special to him, he will smile at you. And things will work out for your good. He doesn't do that to evil people.

"Zara!"

Zara could barely move. She could barely look up to see the rain roaring above her. She could barely see her sister. They had slipped and fallen into the valley below, to be swept away by the waters. Whether by good fortune or bad, they had found themselves wedged into a small boulder by the shore. Alive, and out of the reach of the river. But barely able to move.

"Zara!"

BANG!

"Zara, are you there?! I think I slipped."

Zara said nothing.

"I don't want us to die.' Hauwa cried. "God please…"

I won't die. Don't worry.

"Do you think Daddy will find us?"

He won't.

He did try, to his credit. But he never found them. He'd never find anyone again.

Slowly, Zara started to crawl upward. She barely moved. Blood seeped into the rocks and dripped into the water below. Her head faced upward. Her eyes were on the light above. She tried to raise her hand. If she could only touch that sky, as dark as it was.

"Zara!"

Zara said nothing.

"I think your foot's on my head." Hauwa cried. "Please be careful. I might slip."

BANG!

Zara said nothing.

"Zara?" Hauwa sobbed. "We won't die, will we?"

No. God is smiling on me. I won't die.

KEPRESSNG

The door was locked. She couldn't get out there. She looked around the room for another place to escape. Unfortunately, the only other place she found was the window in the bathroom, which was too high for her to reach. She tried to jump to it from the toilet bowl but fell over and bumped her head on the wall. She lay on the ground, nursing the pain in her head, feeling trapped once more.

I'm going to die. I'm going to die.

I deserve to die. I'm a killer. Killers die.

No, you will not die. I will not die. I won't die today.

God! God!

BANG!

The only option was the door. She would break it down if she had to.

She got to her feet, still rubbing her head, took her bag, and ran to the front door. She grabbed the handle forcefully and pulled it as hard as she could.

It popped open so easily that she nearly fell on her bum.

Meanwhile, it was at the entrance to the police station that Uncle Lateef remembered that his door was no longer locked properly when he happened to see his locksmith reporting a land dispute case at the time. By the time he and his irate friend returned with the policemen as backup, Zara was on a motorbike headed to a place written down in red pen on a sticky note he had carelessly discarded a month ago.

Only Hauwa's father could be buried. Nobody knew what happened that night; it was just that one of the boys found Zara on a rock by the river. No one would ever see Hauwa. Zara couldn't tell them what happened. She knew, but she'd never tell them.

KEPRESSNG

Mama didn't speak when she tended to Zara's wounds. She wouldn't meet her eye either.

The night of the funeral, Zara had her first dream.

Ido bus stop was loud, rowdy, and full of people. It was like the market back at home, even with the people hawking things around the place. The only real difference was the buses. A lot of them. Mostly yellow and black. The last time she'd seen a bus, she had been on one, with the strange woman taking her to that dirty place she slept in before Madam came to pick her up. That one was white and green. And it smelled.

The sun was still not out when Zara stepped down from the bike. She hadn't enjoyed that little trip at all, but she was unable to complain. The side of her head still throbbed.

"Two hundred." The bike man barked. She gave him a thousand naira and stalked off, ignoring the cries for her to return for change. Her bag hung over her shoulder; she clutched the strap like it was her life. Her other hand was buried in the bag, clutching the gun even harder than the other held the bag.

"Benson! Benson! Ido - Benson!"

The bus she headed for was smaller than the one she had used when she came to work for Madam. She couldn't imagine too many people being able to fit in. The conductor hung from the side of the stationary vehicle, yelling his destination to passers-by. Not too many were going from Ido to Benson it seemed.

Zara was hungry. As she headed to the bus, she noticed a white umbrella with a faded yellow square on one side of it. Sitting under it was a kindly young girl roasting corn. She took out some money and approached the corn seller. The corn girl smiled when she saw her. The age difference between them couldn't have been much. It was a lot, but not by much.

"Corn. Corn. Good morning, dear. You want to buy corn?"

Zara nodded.

"You want roasted?"

Zara said nothing. She looked at the girl and pointed to the blackening cobs on her skillet. Zara shook her head.

"You want boiled, abi." The girl said, pointing to a small pot from which steam was pouring out. She reached in and pulled out a golden cob clouded in steam. Zara nodded.

"One. Hundred naira." The girl said.

Three. Zara said, holding out three fingers. The woman pulled out two more corn cobs and put them into salt water.

"You wan buy coconut as well?" The corn seller asked. She smiled warmly at Zara as if she were speaking to her daughter. Zara shook her head. The corn seller packed her corn in a nylon bag and handed it to her. Zara smiled back and handed the money to her. One thousand naira. Zara looked around. A decrepit-looking man sat on the bench beside her, eating corn he hadn't bought. This time, she waited for change.

"Benson! Benson! Benson!" The conductor shouted. Zara took her corn and her bag and approached him. He stared down at her. He wore a permanent frown like a scar, like Aunty Cass. "You dey go Benson?"

She nodded.

KEPRESSNG

"I hope say you get change o. Na two hundred naira."

Zara held up the five hundred and two hundred naira notes in her other hand. The conductor nodded and beckoned for her to enter. A man was already sitting by the door, wearing a shirt folded into his trousers and holding a black Bible. Through some pantomime, she made it known to him that she wanted to sit in the empty space behind him. He obliged her.

She sat at the furthest seat from the front. She didn't wish to be noticed by anyone. The only person sitting close to her was a tall, dark man with long hair. He looked like a shadow, all dressed in black the way he was. He looked the way she felt: scared, sweaty and simply fortunate. He was running away, too. Between them were two chairs that couldn't be used at all. She turned to the window and ate her corn slowly, taking no more notice of him.

She thought of Madam. She thought of her mother. She thought of Uncle Lateef. She thought of the kindly corn seller. She smiled.

The gun was empty now. But it would continue to be useful to her, she knew.

She thought of her home. She would stay there for a few days and leave again. She was a killer now. She didn't belong there.

And luckily for her, she wouldn't make it there, either.

DANIEL ALAKA a writer based in Surulere, Lagos, has a diverse portfolio of unpublished works, including novels, short stories, and screenplays. His short story, The Traitor's Hearing, was shortlisted for the K & L Prize for Literature and subsequently published in the K & L's Histories of Yesterday anthology.

Alongside his writing, Daniel shares his artwork on his Instagram page,

sameasdaniel, featuring his serial comic strips, Virgin Mary.
In his leisure time, he enjoys watching cartoons, listening to music, reading books, and contemplating life.

CONTACTS

Thank you for purchasing this book.
I hope you enjoyed it.
For more, let's meet at any of these places.

Facebook: https://www.facebook.com/kepressng
Instagram: https://www.instagram.com/kepressng
For newsletters: https://www.kepressng.com

OTHER TITLES

Ogu & Other Stories

Notes on Love

Rebirth

Flip-Flop

Oops!

Bound by Fate

Loving Nigeria

ABOUT US

KepressNG (KEP) Ltd proudly stands as an African publishing powerhouse, dedicated to amplifying the influence of African literary creations. Our mission is twofold: to dispel the misguided notion that Africans lack a passion for reading and to champion the diverse voices of African storytellers.

Rooted in our core values of Excellence, Collaboration, Discovery, and Generosity, we are committed to upholding the highest standards in literature and fostering a spirit of community among authors, readers, and publishers alike.

Inaugurating our official opening, we are thrilled to unveil the KepressNG Anthology prize. This prestigious award showcases a curated selection of short stories, showcasing the talent of both emerging and established authors with African heritage. By transforming our vision into a competitive platform, we aim to elevate and expand the landscape of African literature.

Our stories are our legacy, and who better to tell them than us? We recognize the transformative power of storytelling, particularly in shaping the perspectives of young minds. Despite misconceptions about the relevance of short stories, we firmly believe in their enduring significance, especially for young adults embarking on their literary journey.

As custodians of the anthology prize, we are dedicated to reigniting a passion for storytelling and nurturing the next generation of African writers. Through our celebration of African literature, we strive to foster creativity, promote mental well-being, and broaden cultural horizons.

Together, we embark on a journey to build a brighter future for African storytelling, inspiring generations to come with the richness and diversity of our literary heritage.

2026 COMPETITION

Attention all writers of African heritage - this is your moment to shine. The 2026 Kepressng Anthology Prize will officially open for submissions on May 29, 2026. Whether you're a published author or just beginning your journey, we invite you to explore this chance to showcase your talent.

Ten lucky winners will be published in an anthology. This year, the competition features four categories:
~ VINE
~ LILY
~ JUVENILE
~ OAK.

The theme for each category is the same as the title, but it's up to you to interpret it however you wish – literally, figuratively, or creatively.

GUIDELINES
Entry is free and open to all Africans and those of African descent.
~ Your work must be original, unpublished and not AI-generated.
~ Your entry must be in English and fictional.
~ You can submit only one entry per category.
~ All entries must be submitted in MS Word format, double-spaced in TIMES ROMAN font.
~ Your name must not appear in the body of the story.
~ The entry must be between 5,000 and 10,000 words.
~ Your submission email title must be as follows:
CATEGORY TITLE - YOUR STORY TITLE - YOUR NAME (PSEUDONYM).
~ All entries must be received by Midday of October 11, 2026.
~ The winners will be announced six to eight weeks after the last day of submission. (A Change of date will be communicated.)

This is an incredible opportunity to have your work recognised, gain exposure, and most importantly, join a vibrant community of African writers! We can't wait to see your interpretation of these themes.
Send your submissions & FAQs to kemkaezinwo.press@gmail.com.

Good luck.

www.ingramcontent.com/pod-product-compliance
Lightning Source LLC
LaVergne TN
LVHW091633070526
838199LV00044B/1050